"What's going on here?"

Jared mumbled to himself.

The smell of a spaghetti sauce greeted his nostrils. Muscles tense, he scanned the shadows in the living room, grabbed a poker from the fireplace, and stealthily worked his way through the house, determined to find the intruders and boot them out. Someone was setting up house; his suspicions were confirmed by a large tee-shirt and a pair of jeans draped on the stuffed settee in the living room. The master bedroom door was slightly ajar. He moved past it, down the hall, checking each of the other bedrooms. Nothing had been disrupted. Walking back to the living room, he noticed the main bathroom door was shut. Beneath it, the glow of a warm light radiated softly.

Jared grinned. *Caught ya*, he thought.

Drawing his body up to the door and raising the poker, he listened. Not a single sound. Tired of the game, he turned the knob and flung the door wide open.

Nothing!

Confused, he scratched his head. Someone was in the house, or had been recently. The fresh scent of roses coming from the bathroom and the small mounds of bubbles in the tub made it obvious.

He stood back in the hall, and again he noticed the bedroom door. Cautiously, he crept forward. The door flew open with a thud, a woman shrieked.

Was it a woman? *What on earth is on her face?*

"Who are you and what are you doing in here?" he demanded of the green-faced apparition.

Again the woman screamed, but this time she threw a pillow at him as she jumped up from the bed. Flustered, he yanked the door shut.

LYNN A. COLEMAN is a Martha's Vineyard native who now calls the tropics of Miami, Florida, home. She is a minister's wife who writes to the Lord's glory through the various means of articles, short stories, and a web site. She has three grown children and four grandchildren. *Sea Escape* is her first published novel.

Sea
Escape

Lynn A. Coleman

Heartsong Presents

First, I want to thank the Lord for the inspiration. Secondly, to Paul, my hero, my husband of nearly twenty-five years, for his loving support and encouragement. Without him my writing never would have come into being. And last, but not least, I want to thank a very dear friend who helped me fine-tune my writing, Tracie Peterson. To each I say thanks, and I love you all.

A note from the authors:
We love to hear from our readers! You may correspond with us by writing: **Lynn A. Coleman**
Author Relations
PO Box 719
Uhrichsville, OH 44683

ISBN 1-57748-528-9

SEA ESCAPE

Cover illustration by Ron Hall.

PRINTED IN THE U.S.A.

one

Alex's senses tingled from the swirling salty breeze. Perched on the upper deck of the ferry, she leaned forward into the wind, taking in a deep breath. Her nostrils flared at the exotic, briny air. Across the vast expanse of the sea she saw in the distance the land rise before her. Gentle slopes with tawny beaches hugged sandy cliffs crowned with captains' houses. Mated together, they presented a glorious picture of God's handiwork. Never had she seen anything like it. Chilled, she rubbed her bare arms, feeling the sea spray drying on her skin. This was such a different sight from the vast farmlands draped across Kansas.

Martha's Vineyard, a small island off the coast of Massachusetts. Alex smiled. She remembered researching the island in the encyclopedia when she was eight. "You're finally here," she said into the wind, squinting at the sun.

She watched a sea gull gliding alongside the boat. *How can it maintain that speed for so long without a flap of its wings?* she wondered. The gull seemed to be watching her as much as she was watching it. Some small children ran up to the rail, holding out crackers. Alex opened her mouth to correct them, but as soon as she did the gull swooped down and took the treat. The children bounced up and down shouting, "Look at that, look at that, it took it!"

The girl in the trio, maybe around nine Alex guessed, cried out, "Jonathan, let me have a turn!"

"Wait, Sarah!" the older boy asserted himself. "I want to do it again."

Alex snickered to herself as Sarah stood her ground. She swung her hands to her hips and said, "Mom said we *all* could feed the birds."

The older boy seemed to be judging whether or not his sister would tell on him. Reluctantly, he pulled out another cracker and handed it to her. "Here."

The girl's eyes twinkled. She reached out past the rail, standing on her tiptoes. Without hesitation the gull flew to the hand holding out the cracker.

She dropped it.

"See, I knew you couldn't do it," the older boy teased. "Watch me!"

The younger boy meanwhile had figured his own strategy; he grabbed a deck chair and pulled it up to the rail. He asked his brother for a cracker, stood up tall, and thrust his arm out over his head.

Instinctively taking a step forward, Alex wanted to grab the boy from the rail. He was teetering dangerously over the edge. Or so she thought. Out of the corner of her eye she observed a man, whose hair matched the boys', watching them with paternal intensity. He beamed when the youngest had achieved his quest.

"Daddy, did you see that?"

"Sure did, Timmy. Good job, but it's time to get down, okay? Your mother is waiting for us."

"Okay."

The little girl pouted, "I got scared and dropped mine."

Alex watched the interchange between father and children. A smile curled her lips, but a dull ache of longing buried deep within struggled to the surface. Would she ever have children of her own? *Oh Lord, how long do I have to wait? How soon will I come to terms with the fact that I'm not to have a husband or children of my own? Isn't that why I'm still single, Lord?*

"Daddy, can I try again?"

"Sure, one more time. Jonathan, give your sister another cracker."

"That's no fair, I get another cracker too," the younger boy protested.

The girl stood tiptoe, right hand on the rail, the other arm stretched out. A gull swooped in from her right for its treat. The young girl's eyes bulged with expectancy.

Plop! "Eww, Daddy, the bird pooped on me!"

Alex laughed out loud. Bridling her laughter, she turned so as not to embarrass the child.

The boat's horn blasted mere inches from her. She jumped at the spine-jarring assault and covered her ears. Realizing they were entering Vineyard Haven harbor, she decided to make her way down below to the car. Scanning the sky for any more miscreant birds, she headed for the nearest bulkhead.

Two decks down, she rejoined her car. Every vehicle was packed in bumper to bumper, impossibly tight. She remembered her fear when the stewards kept signaling her to come forward. When she got out she'd gasped, seeing only a four-inch clearance.

Alex opened the door, maneuvering her body sideways, and slid into the driver's seat. Weary after the long drive from Kansas, she moaned and fastened her seat belt. Her only stops along the way had been in Indiana to visit a cousin, and again in New York to visit an elderly aunt.

A year's sabbatical. She sighed. "Lord, You know how much I need this year off just to get my head on straight." *And what better way to relax than to search out my family roots?*

Her thoughts drifted back to her patients. She had left her practice in the care of another pediatric physician. They had worked side by side the whole summer, allowing her patients to meet the new doctor. Many of the children said how they would miss her. Giving hugs and kisses, several whispered, "I love you, Dr. Alex."

Alex brushed a tear from her eye. She was losing perspective. Her own desires to have a family, compounded with working with children day in and day out, only magnified the ticking of her biological clock. Seven years in her own practice, seven wonderful but lonely years.

Even the Bible spoke of taking the seventh year off. No, she knew it was the right decision. Fear and uncertainty about her future loomed in front of her, and yet excitement and a sense of urgency to explore the land and history of her own family roots already seemed to provide the solace for which she searched.

The car rocked as the steel ferry bounced off the pilings. Alex gripped her steering wheel, wondering if the captain had misjudged. She looked at the others around her. No one seemed a bit concerned by the ricocheting off of the pilings, nor with the creaking they made.

Easing her grasp, she settled back in her bucket seat. The noisy cranking of metal cables and the clanging rush of steel chains broke her reverie as the heavy ramp leveled off to meet the ferry's deck. She released her pent-up breath, unaware she had been holding it.

Drivers turned their engines on; she did the same. One by one, passengers drove off the boat. Amazed by the speed of their exit, she kept a sharp vigil, awaiting her turn.

Brad and Phyllis Trainer's directions lay on the other seat. Her friends owned the beachfront property that would be her home for the next year. Noting that the first turn was almost immediate, she scanned over the paper one more time. *When you get to Five Corners, you take a right.*

"Five Corners, what kind of a place is that?"

"Yo!" A man tapped her hood. Alex jerked. "Come on, lady, get a move on." She popped her car into gear and it bucked forward. Her cheeks flushed. She followed the line of traffic down a roped-off path through the parking lot. The street immediately before her continued on, but the sign said, "Do Not Enter." She turned left with the rest of the traffic. Stopping at the intersection, she counted, then snickered at herself. Sure enough, five corners.

Alex relaxed in her seat, turned on the directional, and slowly worked her way forward. There was no traffic light. *How could there be for a five-way?* she reasoned. Besides, the thought of traffic lights certainly would take away from the charm of the area. She drove on, picking up the directions again.

"What?"

Stay on this road following signs for Chilmark; but, when you reach the first bend where there are two signs, both having directions for Chilmark, take the right. This will allow you to stay on State Road. She checked the directions again.

"Phyllis," she complained to her absent friend, "I should have had Brad write the directions. I can't understand these."

Alex continued to drive, certain she was completely lost, when she rounded a bend and saw the signs for the town of Chilmark confirming her progress. *This island's not as small as the encyclopedia made it seem!* Thirty minutes had gone by since she left the ferry.

Phyllis's directions said there would be a huge red buoy marking their street. She slowed. Her tires bit into the dirt road and grumbled along, but her Ford Bronco made relatively smooth work of it, she noted with gratitude. Charmed by the grassy mound growing in the center between the well-worn tire treads, she drove deeper into the woods.

An unfamiliar place, the growing darkness, the week-long travel from Kansas, left her exhausted. She needed a good night's rest, but not until she took a long, hot shower.

Finally pulling up to a saltbox structure, she turned off the engine. Her body vibrated. She got out, stretched her back, hoisted her overnight bag onto her shoulder, and headed up the deck stairs. Brad and Phyllis had talked so often about the pleasure of sitting under the stars on their deck and hearing the surf. Alex now found herself straining to listen for distant breakers. Was the ocean really out there in the darkness?

The gentle rhythm of the waves whispered through the brush, filling her with anticipation for what the morning light would unmask. The smell of salt in the breeze soothed her travel-weary bones. Yes, she was here. She was finally here, to track down the seafaring Captain Luce, the grandfather of Alex's distant grandmother, Elizabeth Luce O'Connor, who'd left the island in 1858 to join the man of her dreams. They had gone west to Kansas to find their fortune with an offer of free land.

In the moonlight Alex counted the silver-gray shingles, two down from the door knob and over three. Pulling the shingle, the silver key plopped into her hand. As she entered the house, Alex tossed the key on the table. Moving into the still darkened hallway, she groped for the wall switch. With the flick of the switch, she quickly found the electrical panel and the breakers for the hot water heater and stove.

In the living room, her hand glided over a tea wagon, the wood well worn from the years. On the top of the wagon lay a white crocheted doily with a complete fine china tea set. The work on the floral pattern, so delicate and intricate, of pink and white apple blossoms with green leaves, was set off with gold leaf on the handle. The cup was extremely thin, almost translucent.

Gently she grasped it, turning it over in her hand. Her eyes widened as she read, *Havilland Limoges, made in England/ France*. From what Alex knew of classic antiquities, she estimated this was made around the 1850s, about the same time her ancestor Elizabeth Luce O'Connor had left the island.

After a brief tour of the Trainer home, she unpacked her overnight bag. She pulled out a long flannel nightgown and went into the bathroom, praying the water was heated. It was and she showered, but she quickly exhausted all the hot water.

Grumbling, she made her way to the kitchen, fixed a cup of tea, and opened the sliding glass door facing the surf. The cool ocean breeze penetrated her robe. She grabbed a woolen blanket folded over a chair in the living room. Snuggling deep into a chaise lounge, her fingers curled around the warmth of the mug, and she sipped her tea.

The stars peppered the sky with shimmering brilliance, and the ocean lured her into tranquillity. She rested her head back, closed her eyes, and drifted between awareness and sleep. Words from her grandfather's journal came quickly to mind. *The sea sings the sweetest lullaby.*

"Aye, Grandpa Luce, I see what you mean." Alex grinned and tried to picture the old sea captain in all his glory. There were no photographs of him, no paintings she had ever seen. And yet she pictured him clearly, skin well-leathered from the sun and sea, a barrel-chested man wearing a deep blue wool coat with large black buttons going down the front, wind-blown brown hair, and a reddish-brown beard.

❧

The morning broke bright and crisp. Alex slithered back under the bed covers. Wrapping the warm blanket and sheet up to her chin, she nuzzled the pillow and tried to stay asleep. The trip from Kansas had taken a week, after all; she deserved a day of rest.

But the nagging sunlight drew her from her cocoon. Once dressed, she made herself a cup of tea and strolled out to the deck. The ocean lay before her in all its glory, the blues and sea-greens meshing with the play of light reflecting off the waves. Alex followed the path from the deck to the shore, and discovered the land fell away abruptly. She was on a cliff. A steep, narrow stairway led down to the beach. The wood, well weathered from salt, was gray with sparkles of silver.

The sun was so bright, the air deliciously warm, that Alex decided to test the September water. "Man, that's cold!" She jumped back to avoid the roll of the next wave. She touched the water with her hand, bringing her fingers up to her lips. A slow smile formed. It was salty, just like the air.

She walked the shore for a while, noticing various shells, stones, seaweed, and sponges. *I'll have to purchase a book that will tell me what all this stuff is*, she thought.

Aimlessly, she headed down the shore, not caring about the time. For once, she had no schedules or appointments to keep. She was free, free to do as she wanted. No longer a med-school student pushing herself, or an intern doing her time. No longer Dr. Alex always on call, always needed by others but never needed intimately. Never needed as a person.

This is going to be an incredible year. Just what the doctor ordered to put my life back on track. . .to accept God's leading about being a single woman. . .to not be jealous or resentful toward my patients who have children—wanted or unwanted ones. Here Lord, I'll learn to relax.

She headed toward home and came upon the boathouse the Trainers had mentioned. Their caretaker was building a boat, she had been told, and now she saw its wooden ribs arched toward the sky like the skeleton of a beached whale. Alex calculated it to be twenty-four feet long and maybe eight feet across at its widest point. The bottom hull was already boarded, plus a couple of rows up the sides. What a lot of work! She pondered the skeleton boat, curious about the man who would want to make such a thing. Surely it would be a whole lot easier just to buy one. She shrugged her shoulders and continued back to the house.

≥•

Over the next couple of days, Alex found the local grocery store, post office, and gas station, the basic necessities of life. A map she had purchased now lay sprawled out across the dining room table. Soft rays from the late afternoon sun slanted through the window onto the map as she plotted her course to Edgartown, where the Vineyard Museum and the old historical society were located. Tomorrow she would go down-island and begin tracking her roots.

After supper, Alex decided on a long bubble bath, something she rarely treated herself to. She poured the scented oils and the thick lather piled high up over the edges of the tub. Slowly, she stepped in. "Hmm," she moaned, "heaven on earth." She slid down under the bubbles, their tiny popping noise bringing a smile to her face. The bubbles, so rich and thick, heaped inches high above her shoulders. She fastened her hair up on her head and lay back, closed her eyes, and relaxed.

The water quickly went cool, however. Alex stomped out

of the tub, dried herself off, and calmed her frustrated nerves. What was it with the hot water in this house?

In her room lay an assortment of frivolous purchases she had made that day—a mud mask to rid oneself of worry lines, cleaners, clarifiers, and an assortment of things she wasn't even sure how to apply. She read the instructions and applied the mask heavily on her face. Wrapped in her robe, she lay on the bed, applied cucumber slices to her eyes, and relaxed.

≈

Jared worked his jeep over the rough mounds of his driveway, mumbling to himself about his need to repair them. Having been off the Vineyard for the past week, visiting family and purchasing supplies for the catboat he was constructing, he was glad to be back home. Next to him on the seat sat his notebook, containing the figures for the craft, which he'd rechecked at the Cotuit historical society. While he loved crafting something with his hands, he liked getting it right the first time.

As he passed through the last thicket of trees, a light to his right caught his attention. "What on earth?" He scanned the dark hillside. Sure enough, someone had a light on in the Trainers' home. He took the right fork just before his cottage and ground his way up the cliff toward the Trainers' house. The house seemed still and undisturbed except for the lights on in the kitchen and master bath.

Concerned the house had been looted in his absence, he crept silently up the deck stairs. Cupping his eyes with his hands, he peered through the sliding glass doors. . .everything looked to be in order. He walked around the side to the kitchen door. Locked. Instinctively he went to the shingle where the key was kept.

"What's going on here?" he mumbled to himself.

The key was missing. Whoever had broken in found the key, he figured. His fingers slid down the door jam, checking, just to be sure, for signs of a forced entry. Flustered and confused, he reached into his pocket and pulled out his own set of keys. Fumbling in the moonlight, he at last produced the one he sought.

The smell of a spaghetti sauce greeted his nostrils. Muscles tense, he scanned the shadows in the living room, grabbed a poker from the fireplace, and stealthily worked his way through the house, determined to find the intruders and boot them out. Someone was setting up house; his suspicions were confirmed by a large tee-shirt and a pair of jeans draped on the stuffed settee in the living room. The master bedroom door was slightly ajar. He moved past it, down the hall, checking each of the other bedrooms. Nothing had been disrupted. Walking back to the living room, he noticed the main bathroom door was shut. Beneath it, the glow of a warm light radiated softly.

Jared grinned. *Caught ya*, he thought.

Drawing his body up to the door and raising the poker, he listened. Not a single sound. Tired of the game, he turned the knob and flung the door wide open.

Nothing!

Confused, he scratched his head. Someone was in the house, or had been recently. The fresh scent of roses coming from the bathroom and the small mounds of bubbles in the tub made it obvious.

He stood back in the hall, and again he noticed the bedroom door. Cautiously, he crept forward. The door flew open with a thud, a woman shrieked.

Was it a woman? *What on earth is on her face?*

"Who are you and what are you doing in here?" he demanded of the green-faced apparition.

Again the woman screamed, but this time she threw a pillow at him as she jumped up from the bed. Flustered, he yanked the door shut.

two

Jared paced the living room, glancing down the hall every few moments. He couldn't believe someone had taken up residence in a vacant house. A woman, no less!

What am I going to do? She must be a homeless person or something. But I can't have her living here in the Trainers' house. He tried to roll the tension out of his shoulders.

The sight of her face plastered in green with cucumber slices placed on her eyes resurfaced in his imagination. He suppressed a chuckle.

❧

Still in shock from the hostile invasion, Alex numbly worked her way to the master bath and washed off the facial. The image of the man with the raised fist and a stick. . .no, it had been something metal. . .*what was it? Who on earth was he?* she wondered.

Alex dried off her face with a thick towel. Too angry to be frightened, she stuffed the towel back on the rack and stormed out of the bathroom.

"What *is* your problem?" She hadn't gotten a good look at him before, but now her anger disappeared, and fear crawled up her spine. The man was huge, his shoulders broad and his pectorals like molded steel. Girding herself against intimidation, she stood rigid, eyeing a hasty retreat if necessary.

"Me! Who do you think you are? This isn't your home, lady. I suggest you pack up your bags and move outta here before I call the cops."

"This *is* my home, at least for the next year. So, who do you think *you* are barging into it?"

"For your information, I'm the caretaker of this place. I know who belongs here, and you don't. Now pack your bags and get out," he stormed, pointing toward the door.

Aware now of who he was, her fear subsided. "For *your* information, Mr. Caretaker," she quipped, "my name is Alexandria Tucker, and I have the permission of Brad and Phyllis Trainer to be in their home for the next year." She planted defiant hands firmly on her hips, watching the bluster fade from his face.

Stunned, the guy is actually stunned, she realized with satisfaction. His facial muscles relaxed from anger and changed into. . .what? Worry? "That's right," she pushed on, "the owners, Brad and Phyllis Trainer. Call them. But get out. I resent the fact that you not only walked right into my home, but marched through it like you owned the place. And what on earth were you thinking, flinging the door open like that? Don't you have a shred of decency in you? Are you some kind of Neanderthal? Do you just do whatever you feel like, not giving any thought or respect to others?"

Her adrenaline was pumping now. She had the upper hand and she knew it. Pleased with her newfound ability to go toe-to-toe with such an Atlas, she fought back a grin. But the thundering pulse in her ears signaled she needed to calm down and gain control.

Heat radiated high in Jared's cheeks. Apparently, this woman knew the owners. On the other hand, a discreet search of the town records could have produced the name of the people who owned the property. He narrowed his gaze on her. Maybe she was simply some very crafty thief. "Look, lady, I don't know who you are or what you're doing here, but I know one thing and one thing for certain: If, and I do mean if, the Trainers were allowing you to stay in their home, they would have called me. Which they didn't do. Which means you are a trespasser. Which means you don't belong here. Now, for the last time, pack your bags and get out."

"What do you mean they didn't call you? I was there when Phyllis placed the call. She left the message on your machine."

Jared took a step backward. He had been away for a week. Maybe there was a message. Maybe this woman was telling the truth. "I need some identification. Do you have a driver's license?"

Alexandria marched into the master bedroom and came out almost immediately. "Here." She jammed her license in his face.

Jared took it from her and held it a foot from his eyes. *Alexandria Tucker, MD.* Renewed heat flushed his cheeks. Brad was a hospital administrator in Kansas. Alexandria's license was from Kansas. Jared's heart sank. "Fine, I'll call them. I guess you can stay until I hear from them."

"Well that's awfully magnanimous of you."

Jared headed for the kitchen door. His shoulders slumped. *Why didn't I check my messages first? Why didn't I knock before entering the house? Why am I always a bull in a china closet?* Frustrated with himself, he held his tongue and left her steaming in the living room.

He worked his way around the back of the house to the driveway. *I should have checked this before storming into the house.* A black Bronco sat in the dark shadows of the trees. Jared squatted behind the car and strained to read the words *Land of Oz* in blue lettering against a panel of white. He let out a deep sigh, frustrated with himself, and shuffled his way through the new-fallen leaves to his truck.

Once home he grabbed his phone and dialed the Trainers'.

Phyllis answered immediately. "Hi, Jared, how's the Vineyard?"

"Fine. I was wondering about. . ." Not wanting to play the part of a fool, he decided to ask about the audacious doctor. "I was wondering about Dr. Tucker."

"She should be there by now." Concern rose in Phyllis's voice. "She is there, isn't she?"

"Yes, I was wondering if she was planning on staying through the winter?" He knew the answer to his question before he asked. He shifted uncomfortably on his feet.

"Definitely. Is there a problem with the house?"

"Nope, the hot water heater element should be in soon, and the other items we spoke about I'll take care of shortly." His eyes scanned the caulk and wood preservative he had purchased before going off the island, piled near the door. Caulking the storm windows would take half a day, applying preservative to the deck, the other half. He wondered how he was going to keep Dr. Tucker off the surface until it was dry.

"Fine, do what you need to do. And if Alex needs anything taken care of, you've got my go ahead."

"I understand."

As if sensing his hesitation, she asked, "Jared, is there a problem with Alex and you?"

He hesitated. "Well, if you must know, I didn't get the message she was coming. I was off the island for a week. Anyway, I saw a light on in the place, and I just sort of marched in to check if you'd been robbed."

"I see. So basically you barged in on Alex?" Hearing a slight chuckle in Phyllis's voice, Jared's face flushed again.

"Uh-huh," he admitted. "I'm really sorry about that. I didn't mean to cause a problem." Jared raked a hand through his hair.

"I'm sure she'll get over it. She's a good friend, Jared. Her family actually hails from the Vineyard. I think you'll like her." Phyllis wasn't holding back her laughter now as she said good-bye.

Jared hung up the phone. *Man, I'm such an idiot! But I didn't get the message*, he justified himself.

❦

Alex answered the phone on the first ring. Expecting it to be Jared with an apology, she was surprised to hear Phyllis on the other end. "So, you had a surprise visitor tonight."

"What kind of a man is that?" Alex sat down on the bed.

"An embarrassed one, I'd say. So tell me what happened. It *is* his job to care for our property, you know. I'm sure he thought it was being robbed or someone had set up housekeeping."

"I suppose. But, Phyllis," Alex lamented, "I was lying on the bed with my face plastered with green goo and cucumbers!" She set some pillows up against the headboard and made herself more comfortable.

"Green goo! A facial mask?" Phyllis stifled a giggle.

"It's not funny." Alex fought back a grin.

Phyllis's laughter filled Alex's ear. "He's gorgeous, isn't he?"

"Stop it, Phyllis." Alex remembered the hulk of a man who had stood before her in the living room. "I can't believe how big he is," she admitted. "Is he on steroids or something?"

"Nope, it's all him. He works hard. I've seldom seen him when he wasn't working. Well, that's not quite true. There was a time, once. . ." Phyllis's words drifted off.

"What do you mean, 'There was a time once?' "

"Nothing. Look, he's a great guy, Alex. Give the man some slack."

"Fine, but he's not going to be allowed to just walk in the

place whenever he feels like."

"Alex," Phyllis said, still giggling, "the place is yours. You set up the ground rules. He will need to get in there from time to time to take care of some things for us but you'll work that out with him."

"Just as long as he understands, where I come from people are civilized. We knock on a door before we enter."

When they had said their good-byes, Alex replaced the phone on the nightstand. She thought back on the conversation. Phyllis's comments on how handsome Jared was brought his image to her mind. He was handsome. His blond hair with dark highlights and his dark blue eyes. . .the massive chest, thick arms, and hands. . .Most of the men she knew were slightly built. Seldom had she run across someone who obviously worked out. Pediatrics wasn't the place for well-honed bodies, and few fathers brought in their sick children. Most of the doctors she worked with could hardly be called well-developed. Several were trim, but in a lean sort of way.

Alex grinned as she realized Jared's build was much the same as Arnold Schwartzenegger's in the movies where he played an ordinary guy. He was quite a contrast to herself and her tall, thin frame. Next to him she would appear small and fragile, whereas at the hospital she held her own with the men. Jared certainly had a way of making his presence known.

Picturing him again as he had stood in the doorway of the bedroom, and his accusatory tone, only bolstered her resolve to keep her distance from this guy. Phyllis might find him an excellent caretaker, but he wouldn't be taking care of her, she resolved. Despite how handsome he was, she wouldn't cross that barrier. Nope, Jared was definitely a man to stay away from.

Besides, this was the year she had set aside for growing closer to God and finding His plan for her life. As much as she loved her career, she still ached to have her own family. But time was running out. Her biological clock was ticking, and there were no apparent men standing in line wanting to sweep her off her feet. No, God help her, she needed to get used to the idea she would be single the rest of her life. Maybe someday there might be a man in her life, but certainly no children. "Oh, Father, help me be content with Your plan for my life. Help me trust in You, not in a man, for my happiness. Help heal the ache in my heart for children, family, and my own home. Help me, Lord; I don't know that I can do this alone."

With the fleeting prayer still on her lips, Alex settled under the covers and allowed sleep to help ease the aching in her heart.

∂♣

The next morning Jared paced back and forth in his small kitchen. He had to apologize to Dr. Tucker, but how? Arguing with himself, he considered the straightforward approach. The idea of giving her wild flowers as a token of his sincerity was quickly discounted. *No, then she might think I'm interested in her. It's bad enough the woman thinks I'm some sort of Peeping Tom.* He envisioned her coming at him with fire in her eyes. She was beautiful—after she removed the gunk. "Oh, Lord, please take that image away from my memory."

Alexandria Tucker was more than a feisty woman, he admitted to himself. Many women had tried over the years to get his attention but no one had, not since Hannah. "No, I'm just getting my life back on track with You, Lord. I don't need a woman to complicate things. Not now Lord, not now."

He jammed his eyes shut, forcing Dr. Tucker's image out of his thoughts. Raking his hands through his hair, there was nothing left to do but simply go up to the house and apologize. He had made a mistake. That's what it was, a simple mistake. *How was I supposed to know she was coming?* Which made him wonder when the Trainers had decided to let Dr. Tucker stay in their home—and why.

With large ground-gaining strides, he worked his way up over the rise. The distance between his place and the Trainers' was minimal, good for the lungs. A brisk pace set, he trudged up through the beach grass. The view from this area was breathtaking, but Jared refused to take the time to admire God's handiwork. He had a job to do and it was time to get it over with, no matter how uncomfortable it was.

Taking the back steps, two at a time, up to the kitchen, he reached for the door and knocked. Seeing her fully clothed and in the kitchen, he marched straight in.

three

"Dr. Tucker. . ."

Alex cut him off. "Don't you have any social graces at all?"

"I came to apologize." A sarcastic retort would have been easier.

"Fine, but who do you think you are? You just walked right into my house, again."

"I knocked."

"While you were already opening the door. You might have waited for a response. Did you grow up in a barn?"

"Whoa, Doc, hold it. Number one, I noticed you were in the kitchen. Number two, what's your problem?"

Alex was about to protest, but he wasn't going to let her have the last word today.

"There's no need for sarcasm. Henceforth I will gladly await your precious response before entering your home. However, I do have to work on this place."

"No sarcasm, huh? You can do your precious work, anytime I'm not around. I don't take kindly to people just barging in on me. You've done it twice now. I'll not stand for it another time."

"Fine, it won't happen again." He took a step back, reaching for the door.

"Fine."

Jared stormed out of the house. *Boy, that went smooth, Madeiras. Maybe you should try again. Yeah right, and get my head chopped off by the wicked witch of Kansas. No, thank*

25

you very much! He bristled all the way to the boathouse.

He needed to work. He needed to expend some energy. Verbal boxing matches with the pretty doctor was not his idea of a good time. No, this was time to work hard, work off his frustration, and most important work off his anger.

He hadn't been this mad at anyone since releasing his anger toward God about the death of Hannah, the one woman he had loved. The one God took away days before their wedding. He was young then, only twenty-two, but no one since had ever come close to her. She was his soul mate, God's choice for him—and yet before they became husband and wife, God took her away.

His fist slammed the stern of the boat. *No, God, I don't want to remember that. I don't want to remember the pain. It's over, let it die!* Emotional shutdown had been his answer. He refused to allow it to hurt any longer. Hannah was dead. There was no future for them. He ground his teeth and went to work firing up the steam baths; he needed to soak the wood before he could begin.

❧

Alex threw the frying pan into the sink. *Just who does that man think he is!* She huffed out loud, willing herself to calm down. *Why does he rile me so?*

Thoroughly exasperated with her own behavior, her self-confidence in herself as the calm, level-headed sort was shaken. *For Pete's sake, I've dealt with aggravating people every day at the hospital. . .egotistical colleagues, or worse yet, money-grabbing colleagues, who don't care one hoot about their patients. So why can't I handle some country bumpkin?* Her reputation in the medical field stood for control and discipline, someone not easily irritated. This reaction to Jared was not normal. Not for her, anyway. She needed to take a more professional approach.

"Later, I'll think about this later," she muttered at the ceiling. "Today, I'm going to begin my search for Grandpa Luce."

Heading into the dining room, she pulled out her map of the Vineyard and reviewed her course to the historical society, deciding to pick up South Road at Bettlebung Corners to the Edgartown-West Tisbury Road. They were the island's back roads, but they still seemed the most direct route. Being the tourist area it was, streets were well marked. A bunch of purple grapes in the upper center of the state road signs made them easy to recognize.

Alex grabbed her keys, map, and purse, and headed into her family's past. "Oh Lord God, make this a better day than it's started out so far," she prayed as she bounced out the dirt path now familiar as the Trainers' driveway.

As she drove past the Chilmark Library and Community Center, she turned onto roads she hadn't yet traveled. She passed a small pond on her left, decoratively laced with swans and ducks. Her tires squealed as she rounded a big bend in the road that curved to the left at almost a complete right angle. Stone walls lined both sides of South Road. On her right past the open fields were ponds, and then sand dunes and beach grass looking out over the ocean. The view was breathtaking.

A horn blared, bringing her attention back to the road. "Alex, old girl, you'd better keep your eyes on the road. The surf will be there another day." She calculated the next time she could come back around here and take in the view. "Relax, you've got a year. You've only been here a handful of days."

Easing back into her bucket seat she continued her trip. Noting the sign for the fairgrounds in West Tisbury, she decided to make that another place she would have to stop. Her eye caught a strange sight: an artist had turned his yard into an outdoor exhibit. Alex smiled. Life on the Vineyard was not going to be boring. There were plenty of new things to explore and find.

Alex pulled onto the grass outside the Vineyard Museum and tucked her map between the seats. Grabbing her purse and other items, she marched through the white-gated fence. In front of her was a truncated lighthouse. After reading the information on the plaque, stating that it was in fact the actual top to the old Gay Head lighthouse, she went inside and looked at the prisms. *Amazing,* she thought. Simple lantern lights, fueled with whale's oil, refracted through the prisms to warn the ships of old. She pictured her Captain Luce depending on them to warn him of the rocks and shoals. Alex marveled at the realization that light is still measured in terms of candle power, one lumen equaling one candle.

As she made her way to the back of the property she came upon an open structure with various sleighs, boats, and wagons. Three lone gravestones stood near the building. Wondering who was buried at the historical society, she meandered over to read the markers. "Chicken tombstones?" she chuckled. "Someone buried chickens? Oh no! It was a Luce, a Nancy Luce. I wonder if we're related? She called them her 'beloved chickens.' Unbelievable!" She snickered and made her way to the main building. The library and gift shop were located inside.

The historical librarian, Beatrice Arno, was quite helpful, pulling out logs and journals that Captain Thomas Luce had written. Alex had a transposed copy that one of her great-aunts had passed on to family members years ago, which eventually got passed down to her. That was probably the key item that spurred her on to further her knowledge about the sea and Captain Luce. Now she could see the originals.

She spent hours poring over the information. A map of Holmes Hole, 1858, now known as Vineyard Haven, a village of Tisbury, was shown to her. She found her grandfather's home on Main Street, north of Church Street and on the harbor side of the road.

"Excuse me, can you tell me how I can locate this house?" She pointed to the spot on the old map.

The older woman with snow-white hair placed her glasses high on the bridge of her nose and leaned over the map. "Oh, I'm sorry, Miss, but that house was burned down in the Great Fire of 1883. There's another home on that spot, I believe. Let me check who it belongs to."

"No, that's okay." It wouldn't be the house her adventurous ancestor had been raised in. She had left the Vineyard in 1858 with her new husband bound for Kansas. Alex's excitement about possibly seeing her ancestor's home sank into quiet disappointment.

"I'll be glad to help you with some more research on Captain Luce and that time period if you wish."

"Definitely, I'll be back. Tell me, did everyone go to sea back then?"

The woman nodded. "There's an oral history by Stan Lair, and he talks about every male in Vineyard Haven going to sea at one time or another."

"Makes sense." Alex thumbed the old leather diary lying beside her. "Back then the sea was the primary income of the island."

The woman nodded again. "There were some farmers of course, some factory work but mostly the ocean was their provider."

"Whaling?"

"Primarily yes, but the whaling industry was ending about that time. Oil had been discovered and westward expansion was being encouraged."

"I know. I'm from Kansas. My ancestor left the island with her new husband for the promise of land and wealth."

Beatrice gave her a knowing smile and told her a little about some of the historical sites she could find in Edgartown; the old Whaling church, the Sculpin Museum, the row of captains' houses. Alex decided a walking tour of Edgartown in the bright afternoon would be in order. Leaving her car parked outside the museum, she headed to Main Street and up a little on her left to the old Whaling church. There was no way to mistake it. The huge white columns out front stood a couple stories high.

ঝ

A sheen of sweat covered Jared's body, not only from his labor, but also from running the steam baths. Soaking the wood softened it for curving against the ribs of the hull. Steaming sped up the process. The last boat he made had been modern, using molded fiberglass. Actually, it had been a replica of an ancient vessel rumored to have crossed the Atlantic. But this new boat was going to be something quite different, a catboat, used on the cape for fishing. The low draft was built exclusively for use on the shoals of the cape and islands. The men could drag scallop dredges, rake for quahogs, or go into deep water to fish for cod. They even pulled up lobster pots with them. In other words, it was a great multi-purpose boat for the area.

Finding the wood from area trees had been his hardest assignment. The cape and the islands no longer had the amount of trees needed to support a wood mill. Getting wood grown the closest to the area the boat would be used in was best for protection from the various sea worms and other wood-eating critters.

Jared ran his rough, callused hand over the area he had been sanding. Originally his plan had been to build the boat in the same way they had been made in the mid-1800s. However, the many hours of hand sanding versus power sandering was an allowance he decided to fudge on. The ridge between the seams felt smooth. Content with its appearance, he placed the sander down beside him on one of the supports holding the frame of the boat in place.

He unrolled the blueprint of the catboat across his workbench and checked and rechecked his work, since details, all the details, were important. The copy of his plans had come from the Cotuit historical society. The Cape Cod town had been one of the largest builders of catboats during the mid- to late 1800s.

Jared had decided on a twenty-four foot vessel. Large enough for a cabin so he could make an occasional sail out to Nantucket or Block Island. He placed a small piece of oak on the upper right hand corner of the pages, while his left arm held down the opposite side.

He smiled; she was coming along well. Jared lifted his left arm and the plans curled over the block of oak. "Name. . . what shall I name you?" he pondered, scanning the boat from bow to stern. The name *Alexandria* leaped up in his head. He snickered. "I don't think so. Alex isn't a controllable woman. You will be controlled by me—the captain!"

Jared pulled the now cold mug of coffee toward him. "The poor man that marries that woman." He wondered if Phyllis and Brad knew how bossy and hard that woman could be. *Doesn't matter anyway, she's their friend and she's going to*

be here for the better part of a year, old boy, so get used to it.
Raising the mug the rest of the way, he took a sip. It was
cold and bitter; one sip was enough. He placed the mug back
on the workbench.

The sound of an approaching car drove him out of the boathouse and around to the back of the building. "Jared, old
boy, when did ya get back?" called a man's voice.

"Last night." Jared smiled. John Poole was an old dear
friend. A friend to his parents, a man that stood by him when
Hannah and his parents were killed. John had been on the
water since before he could walk, and had more saltwater
running in his veins than Jared did. He'd worked on his family's fishing boat since he was old enough to spit. A small
gold earring looped through his right earlobe. John had it
long before it was a fashion statement. In fact, the gold earring was a seaman's badge of honor.

"What brings you out here?" Jared asked.

"Wondering what's going on with your fancy new neighbor."

"What do you mean?" Jared questioned with a smile.
Apparently nothing escaped the island gossip lines.

"Pretty thing. A doctor, I've heard tell, from Kansas."

"That's about all I know. She's a friend of the Trainers and
they gave her the run of the place."

"Heard her say she was researching her family roots—
claims to be a descendant of Captain Thomas Luce."

"You know more than I, John."

"You mean a pretty thing like that walks by you and you
haven't noticed her?"

"I noticed but I'm not interested."

"Well, I'll be squid for dinner. If I was forty years younger
I'd ask her out myself."

"She's all yours John. Let me warn ya, she's got a temper."

"Oh does she now?" John's white bushy eyebrows rose high on his forehead.

Jared shifted his weight uncomfortably. "You want to help me with the catboat?"

"Of course. Don't think I left Martha's good cooking just to check into your love life, do ya?"

Jared wanted to protest that he didn't have a love life, but he knew John would get the best of him and not let it drop. "Come on, I'll show you what I found," Jared said instead, placing his arm around John's shoulder.

The man had become the grandfather he'd never known. John understood him like no other. Smiling, he led him to the bench and showed him the antique brass compass, winches, and other assorted treasures.

ð

Inside the church, Alex noticed the old wooden floors, the floorboards wide and thick. The pulpit was off to the side on a small raised platform. The pews were huge; she couldn't recall ever seeing any with that wide of a seating area or any as long. In her mind she pictured a preacher standing up front preaching about the dangers of the sea and how a man ought to be right with God before he left the harbor.

The ninety-two foot clock tower was said to be visible far out to sea, according to a brochure she acquired. All and all it was an impressive building, showing the money the whaling industry had brought to this area. The church was built in 1843, fifteen years before her Grandma Elizabeth left the island. Alex wondered if she had ever attended this church. It was possible, but having learned that her relatives primarily lived in another town she thought it was doubtful.

Alex left the church and headed down Main Street toward the harbor, musing how communities reflected their people by size of houses and the intricacies built into the houses or structures. She marveled that she was walking on brick sidewalks, very old and very worn red bricks.

At the base of Main Street was a parking lot, and the Edgartown Yacht Club sat on a wooden pier. Turning left onto Dock Street, she worked her way to the Chappy Ferry, a small three-vehicle flat barge that crossed back and forth across the harbor. "Chappy," she quickly learned, was the local nickname for the small island of Chappaquidick on the other side of the Edgartown harbor.

The swirl of the tide rushing past made the water appear dangerous. The only other time she had seen water moving that fast was at a river that often sported white water rafting. Reading the name *On Time* on the ferry, she sat on a bench watching it and getting a feel for the harbor. This was one of the main whaling harbors of the past. Chappaquidick, on the other side, helped to enclose the harbor. Behind her sat the Old Sculpin Gallery with a whaling boat on the grassy lawn.

She tried to visualize how the scene must have looked back in the 1800s. The gallery, she read, made whaling boats right there. In fact two of the them were now in the Smithsonian. The fine hairs on Alex's neck stood on end as she realized just how much history was in this area.

After spending some time in the gallery, she made her way up Daggett Street, up the hill to North Water Street where the row of captains' houses still stood. She stared at the widows' walks, picturing wives looking out to sea, waiting for their husbands' return. She looked for doorways that would lead onto the widows' walks and failed to see one. Noting the area, she decided to find a captain's house she could tour. She thought back to her Captain Thomas Luce and wondered if his wife had a widow's walk too, if she had fretted for the return of her husband. Alex shook her head, recalling that an average whaling trip lasted three to four years in the 1800s.

At one point on North Water Street there was a break with no house on the opposite side of the street, closest to the harbor. The view was breathtaking. . .the green of the sea grass, with small patches of beach sand, the water, a white lighthouse glistening in the sun. The top of the light was painted black.

She looked at her watch, then returned to Main Street, following North Water Street. A small group of tourists stood outside a store window. Alex's curiosity was piqued. She stopped and watched. The place was called Murdock's Fudge, and the confectioner was making the largest batch of fudge she'd ever seen. In front of him was a long, narrow table with a marble top. The fudge was folded over and over again upon itself.

The temptation was too great. Alex stepped into the shop. In the glass case were many varieties of fudge. She picked chocolate with walnuts, then noticed a pink fudge with red berries inside. The sign read cranberry fudge. The woman behind the counter gave her a small sample. Alex decided to add some cranberry fudge to her purchase. *Well, it wouldn't be right to pass up items unique to the area*, she justified.

Fudge in hand, she continued back to her car. The shops, the street, the area had too much to offer for one single afternoon. Finding the museum and her car were simple feats, but driving through the one-way streets to the Edgartown-West Tisbury Road challenged her internal compass. She soon made it, however, and headed back up the island to her home away from home.

At the house she thumbed through the pages of an island history and folklore book she had recently purchased and looked up Edgartown. The area excited her. No wonder it was so popular with tourists. The setting was beautiful, the shops quaint, the people friendly, and everything was so packed with history. The Vineyard actually had some of the oldest towns in the United States.

Thomas Mayhew founded the town of Edgartown in 1642. In hopes of gaining favor with the king, he had named it after the three-year-old son of King Charles I. However, unbeknownst to Mayhew, the boy had died the month before.

Closing the book, Alex made herself some dinner.

≥

Jared's stomach knotted when he heard Alexandria pull into the Trainers' drive. Torn, he debated with himself. Should he attempt another apology?

"Why bother?" he muttered.

On the other hand, if she had found favor with the locals, maybe he'd just caught her on a bad day. He shook his head. *No, she can just stay right there, I'm keeping to myself.* Ambling back to the blueprints, he scanned over them once again. His concentration, however, was almost nil.

A late afternoon delivery brought the needed part to fix the hot water heater, and again he found himself in debate. He really should repair the heater for her.

Maybe a cold shower or two will help to calm that woman down, he thought. *And then she'd have to come to me about the repairs.* That thought stirred up a sense of false pride. He snickered at himself, and set the part down to make his dinner. It could wait until morning. *Besides, she told me not to come except when she was not around*, he justified as he nuked another frozen dinner in his microwave. A lukewarm shower would be fine for her. It wasn't like she would catch a cold from it.

Irritated that someone was living so close to him, he shuffled his way through his cottage. He got along with the Trainers, but they had their own lives, their own set of friends. Jared rarely ever saw them. This woman, however, was a bother. Not only did she have a low opinion of him, not that it bothered him, but she also was disturbing his thoughts.

The entire day. . . Where she was—what she was doing. No! He had to stop this! He didn't like it. Not one bit.

"How can one woman be so. . .fascinating?"

Bewildered, he forced himself to stop thinking about her. "Lord, please help me here. My mind is exhausting me."

four

The day's sweat, dirt, and salt on her body made Alex yearn for a long hot shower. She hoped the hot water heater would provide the needed warmth. The few baths and showers so far had been lukewarm.

Standing in the bathroom, she reached into the stream of water and set the temperature. It seemed warmer, she thought as she stepped into the shower. Under the pulsing stream she relaxed. Lathering up her hair she leaned back to rinse.

The water started getting colder. Irritation flared its ugly head. She snapped off the cold water faucet. Tepid was the best she could call the water temperature.

Gritting her teeth, Alex rinsed her hair. Quickly, she scrubbed her body from the top of her head to the bottom of her feet. Showers this short belonged to her college days, when she'd always been in a hurry to get to class, having overslept due to a late night of studies.

She turned off the now cold water, teeth chattering, and dried herself off. "I need to call a plumber. I can't live like this," she muttered on her way to the bedroom.

Once dressed, she placed a call back home to Brad and Phyllis. Brad informed her that Jared was well aware of the problem and had to order the part needed for the repairs. The idea of approaching that man for anything was not very appealing, however. Granted, he was a sweet diversion to her eyes, but the gall of the man was something she just couldn't tolerate. Besides, it was late. There was no need to contact him this evening. No, she'd wait until morning.

She browsed through the various books Brad and Phyllis had in their library. One in particular caught her attention. *Lost at Sea*, by J. Madeiras. The back cover revealed that the author had been attempting to cross the Atlantic when his ship, caught in a bad storm, capsized and left him stranded in the elements for eight days.

A good book would be a perfect distraction. The image of the handsome but annoying caretaker weighed too heavily on her mind. Alex seized the book and brought it eagerly into the living room. She lounged across the couch, tossing a lap blanket over her legs.

Opening to the dedication, she read, *To those I've lost. They will never be replaced, nor will my love for them be diminished.* Alex's heart tightened. She wondered who had died, and if they had perished on this tragic journey out to sea. She turned the page and began to read.

The man was educated, she realized right off by the words he chose. And he has a sense of humor, she smiled, nuzzling deeper into the soft folds of the couch. This was going to be a good read.

જ

Jared woke with the sun, far from rested. Dr. Alexandria Tucker had plagued him all night. He really had gotten off on the wrong foot with the woman and needed to apologize. If not that, he needed at least to calm the storm brewing between them. She didn't need to come begging for his help. He was being childish about the hot water heater. Chastising himself for his behavior, he decided to make peace with his neighbor.

He grabbed the heating element and hiked up the hill to the Trainers' home. The smell of bacon filled the air, and his stomach grumbled. He knocked on the door and waited.

There she was, pretty as a three-masted schooner with her sails full and the waves rolling down her sides. Her mouth was tight, almost tense, he assessed. She wasn't looking forward to seeing him, and he knew why. "Dr. Tucker, I came by to fix the hot water heater. May I come in?"

Alex opened the door to him.

"Thank you. It won't take me too long."

"Did Brad call you?"

"No, is there a problem?"

"No, I called him last night about the hot water heater. He told me that you were aware of the problem and I should speak with you."

So, she was avoiding him as much as he was avoiding her. "I'm afraid I need to drain the heater before I can replace the heating element."

"No problem, do what you need to do. I like my hot water."

Jared smiled, then quickly removed the smile. He was gloating. Obviously, she had had a miserable shower or bath, lukewarm at best. "I'm sorry. I could have come by last night, but I. . ."

"It's okay. I think we both needed a night to cool off."

He hesitated, then sucked in a deep breath. "Dr. Tucker, I'm sorry about walking in on you. I really was just concerned about the Trainers' belongings. They have many valuable antiques."

Her face softened. "I know. I overreacted. I'm sorry. Shall we begin again?"

"I'd like that."

"Me too. Did you have breakfast?" she asked.

He shook his head. "But I wanted to fix your hot water heater immediately." He eased his breath out slowly.

"I've got plenty of food. Would you care to join me?"

He shrugged. "Thanks, don't mind if I do. Let me start draining the tank and I'll be back."

Alex went to the kitchen and added some bacon to the frying pan.

Maybe we can be neighbors after all, Jared thought as he went outside to get the hose. Ten minutes later he was wiping his hands on a cloth, joining her in the kitchen.

"Smells great."

"Thanks, it's just bacon and eggs."

"There's nothing 'just' about bacon. It has to be one of my favorite meats."

Alex laughed, the first laugh he had heard from her. The lilt of her laughter flooded his senses. This was a mistake, he realized; it was better if she were his enemy.

He sat down wearily at the table, while he closed down his heart and his emotions. No one would ever be allowed to enter it again. He had lost too many people in his life. He couldn't deal with the pain of any more loss. Resolute in his conviction, he fired off a quick prayer, murmuring his thanks to God for the meal, and then he forked the eggs into his mouth.

Her head was bowed in prayer, he saw. *For pity's sake, she's a believer too! Lord, what kind of test are You putting me through?*

❧

Alex wolfed down her breakfast in fierce determination to leave the house as soon as possible. Jared's presence in the house awakened desires in her that long had been under control. As a doctor she understood chemistry. This, however, didn't make sense. Never in all her days had she been attracted simply by the way a man looked.

Well, maybe when she was a teen in high school and a certain rock and roll star had caught her interest. How her mother ever tolerated her placing all those pictures on her bedroom wall she would never understand. When she had grown past that phase her father had to repaint the wall. All the tape marks, missing paint, and various holes from tacks and small nails had made it appear like a scatter bomb had gone off. But that was her only time for such foolishness, and after all, that was puberty; it was only natural.

This however, was different, strange, and completely unnerving. No, Jared needed to work, and she needed to clear her head. She jumped up and placed her plate in the sink. She realized she had been a bad hostess, not offering a single word of conversation during breakfast. "Sorry to eat and run, Jared," she blurted. "I need to get some errands done."

His gaze pierced right through her. He knew she was uncomfortable, she sensed, but thankfully, he couldn't read the thoughts she had been having, thoughts about how his arms might feel wrapped around her. No, it was certainly better he didn't know that! She was too vulnerable. Hadn't she just left home to find herself, to make peace with God's plan for her to remain single the rest of her life? After all, time was running out, there was no way she would be having children, a husband, a happy life ever after. No, she was being called to be single.

True, she hadn't heard a definite word from God on the matter, but she would be silly not to realize His purpose when He had not seen fit to provide the man she had been praying for since she was thirteen. That was twenty-two years ago. Here she was thirty-five and acting thirteen. Goodness, she didn't need this now.

"Thanks for fixing the hot water heater," she murmured.

"Welcome, have a good day." His mutter was equally terse.

Escaping back into her bedroom, she grabbed her purse, keys, and a sweater. "Time to explore the island," she called to him as she stood by the door, tossing the keys around her finger into the palm of her hand.

She heard him in a back room, and she wasn't certain he had heard her. No, she wasn't going to go find him and tell him good-bye. She thrust herself out the door. Fresh air, the smell of the salt, calmed her nervous reactions. She paused and took a deep breath. She was being silly.

Silly or not, she did want to take in the sights. A trip to Gay Head and the clay cliffs was on her agenda for the day.

❧

Jared replaced the hot water heater in record time. Alex's obvious uneasiness with him gave him a resolve that the next time he was to see her he would go out of his way to be nice. There was no sense having the lady afraid of him.

Back at the boathouse, he fired up the steam baths again for the day. An hour later, he removed the steaming planks that would make up the sides of his boat. Setting each one in place, he hammered it to the ribs. They curved nicely against the frame.

The day was unseasonably warm, and the steam from the baths added to the heat. Removing his shirt, he continued to work. It was a long process, something that wouldn't be a problem if he'd simply gone out and bought a boat like most people.

His compulsion to build things with his hands had been with him ever since he could remember. His father was a similar man, and rumor had it, so was his grandfather. Having built his own boat before he had left the family, his grandfather had sailed for parts unknown after an argument with his wife.

Jared's father, Michael, was left with the impression that the man simply ran out on his family. Michael Madeiras quit school and went to work to support his mother, brothers, and sisters. He was the oldest, so it was his responsibility. He started working as a fisherman, but the pay wasn't very good. He went to work for a contractor, then finally went out on his own. By then the rest of the siblings were grown. He fell in love and married Jared's mother. They were a good match; she mirrored his stubborn streak with her own brand of tenacity. They worked through their differences and stayed united in their efforts to raise their children.

His father was a good man, a man Jared was proud of. In fact, the only thing his parents had ever done that really bothered him was when they had gotten themselves killed in a freak accident when a deer had leapt in front of their car.

Jared's throat tightened. They were gone. Hannah was gone. He accepted those facts. He just didn't know why God hadn't prevented it, why He had chosen to take away the people from his life he cared about most. It didn't make sense. Not when others he had grown up with still had their parents, when the same people were allowed to marry their sweethearts. It just didn't seem fair.

But spending those eight days at sea, Jared had learned a little bit about God's fairness. At the same time, he had found that he was a fighter and didn't want to die. He accepted that freak things, such as storms, unexpected deer, and aneurysms, happened in this life. He had made his peace with God. But he wasn't ready. . .no, he would never be ready to open his heart to another. The pain of the loss was too much to bear. He couldn't, he wouldn't, go through that again.

The image of Dr. Alexandria Tucker and the lilt of her laughter flooded over the darkness of his thoughts. She was beautiful, and what a captivating smile! But she was afraid of him. It didn't make sense. If he were some kind of deviant, wouldn't he have harmed her that first night? Why didn't she see the logic in that argument?

He left the boathouse and walked down to the shore. The gentle roll of the waves lapped the edges of his work boots. He squatted down, sitting on his haunches, then picked up small stones and shells, tossing them into the water. He was a good man, an honorable man. No one ever before had been afraid of him. He made her nervous, though; how was he going to handle that? "Lord, I don't want to frighten the poor woman, but I can't exactly allow her too close. Her beauty, her mannerisms, disturb me as if I were a teenager all over again. What can I do to change things?"

A wash of calming peace rushed through him. In his mind he felt as if God were saying to simply wait and give her time to get to know him for who he really was.

"I reckon I can wait, Lord."

&

Alex scanned the clay cliffs in front of her. They were so different from the pictures she had seen of them many years ago. A large red cliff that should have been in the foreground was missing. She looked to the shoreline below and saw the sea was full of red clay. Of course, she pondered, erosion must have taken its toll on the red cliff. The remaining cliffs were beautiful hues of whites and yellows, some with a hint of green. She scanned the short distance from the edge of the cliffs to the bottom of the Gay Head lighthouse and wondered how many years it had left to stand in its present position before erosion would relentlessly lay its claim. This lighthouse was so different from the one in Edgartown. It was painted brown for one thing, and the rail up on top was black.

She stopped in the little shops the local Indians maintained to rid tourists of their money. In spite of herself, she bought some trinkets for her friends and family, and with her arms full of bundles, she headed toward the car. The view before her, running down the south side of the island, took her breath away. . .the large rocks lining the shore and protruding from the water, the bright white sand that made up the beach. Green bushes lined the way back to the paved road.

She turned her attention toward the north side of the island. The air was so clear she could see across the bay to Chilmark, probably right to the area where the Trainers' home was.

She had been wrong to clam up this morning with Jared, she realized as time and distance gave her a better sense of perspective. She had made Jared uncomfortable, as well as herself. She needed to rectify that situation upon her return.

She placed the items in the back of her Bronco and got in, not certain how she was going to ease the situation between her and Jared. As she made her way home, she discovered a few small buildings that made up the town of Gay Head.

After the car was unloaded she headed toward the boathouse, assuming she would find Jared there. Along the path to the boathouse, on bushes of varying height, she saw some purple berries. Curious, she picked a few and continued down the path. She reached the boathouse and came upon him.

And there he was—all six-foot-one, two hundred and

thirty-five pounds of him. His chest was huge, the muscles on his back and arms playing an alluring, hypnotic dance. Stunned, she stood still and watched. His movements were swift and agile. Med school had never prepared her for a man that looked like this.

He turned and smiled. "Can I help you?"

Alex fumbled for words. "I, I. . ."

"Yes?" His grin was disarming. She sensed he knew what his body was doing to her, and he was eating it up.

"I wanted to apologize for breakfast. I—I wasn't very talkative, I guess."

"No need to apologize. I know you don't think highly of me. I'm sorry."

"It's not that." What was it that made her feel so nervous around him?

Jared grabbed a rag and wiped off his hands.

"I'm just a little uncomfortable around you." If he only knew how uncomfortable, she would be at the mercy of this man. She couldn't let that happen. "Thanks for fixing the hot water heater."

"Not a problem."

Alex felt the berries in her hand. *That is a safe subject,* she thought. "Can you tell me what these are?"

Jared stepped closer and held her hand in the inside palm of his huge masculine grip. Her body almost gave her away as she felt her fingers start to tremble, but she caught herself and kept them still. With his other hand he picked up one of the berries. "These are called beach plums."

"Are they edible?"

"Yes, although you generally make them into jellies, jams, and sauces. The seed is large and the fruit is tart. There is very little of the fruit between the seed and its skin."

"How can I make this jelly? How many of these things would I need to pick?"

"I believe Phyllis picked up a book called *Plum Crazy* a few years back that's filled with recipes."

Alex belatedly realized she had left her hand in his and she jerked it free. She decided to look for the book and attempt to make this local delicacy. "Well, thanks," she said awkwardly.

"Welcome."

Alex rushed away from the boathouse and found the cookbook. She needed ten cups of the berries and two cups of water to make juice for the jelly recipe. Grabbing a container she went back to the bush. The beach plums were plentiful, and within an hour she was done.

She had worn a pair of shorts and a short sleeve blouse while picking. She looked at the scratches from the briars. "I should cleanse the wounds well in order to prevent infection," she murmured to herself.

ਅ

Jared turned off the baths for the evening. The day had been a productive one; he was pleased with how many planks were in place. He thought back on the beach plums Alexandria had picked, and scanning the bush she had probably picked from, he spotted some poison ivy. There were still some leaves but because it was early fall, most of the leaves were off the plants.

He ran down to his house and picked up a bar of Fels Naptha brown soap. *She's going to need to wash with this immediately*, he thought. He ran back up the hill and rapidly pounded on the door.

He saw her approach and smiled when she opened it. "Hey, Doc, did you pick those beach plums yet?"

"Yes, I've got them in the sink. I just rinsed them."

He looked at the scratches on her legs. "I don't suppose you folks have poison ivy out in Kansas, do you?"

five

She narrowed her gaze, knitting her eyebrows together. "What is it you're trying to tell me, Jared?"

"I believe while you were picking the beach plums you probably rubbed up against some poison ivy." He handed her a yellowish-brown bar of soap. "I stopped at the bush where I think you were picking. Please take this soap and scrub with it. It helps!"

Alex had already begun to itch, but she had chalked it up to the scratches. She looked down at her legs. If the poison ivy had gone into her bloodstream she was definitely in for an extreme case of it.

"Alexandria, you're a doctor—can you call in a prescription? I think some cortisone would be in order."

"I suppose I should. I'd better wash."

"Can I get you anything? Go to the drugstore for you?"

"Thanks, maybe I should call in the prescription first." Alex went to the phone and pulled out the local directory. She felt foolish; she should have noticed the poisonous plant.

Jared left after she placed the call, and she went into the bathroom, stripping off her clothes and placing them in the washer first. Once in the shower she scrubbed, thankful the water was finally hot—until she realized the hot water would open her pores, allowing more of the poison to sink into her skin. Groaning, she turned the faucet knobs, knowing she would have to endure a cold shower. She lathered

50

herself twice, then gave herself a final rinse. Teeth chattering, she gave in and turned up the heat.

She set the washing machine and headed into the kitchen, her legs tingling. Unsure if the itch was caused by the poison ivy or the mere thought of it, she attempted to ignore the impulse to scratch. She decided on shorts. Feeling the rub of the fabric against her legs would only increase the desire to scratch.

Jared returned after she was all showered and changed. In his arms was a pizza box and a couple of bags. "I hope you don't mind, but I took the liberty of ordering some pizza for us. I also picked up some calamine lotion to help with the itching. And a few more ointments, all claiming to help."

She gave him a grateful smile. "Thanks, that's really sweet of you."

"How bad are the cuts?" he asked, straddling a chair beside the table.

"Not very deep, but they sting. I honestly didn't see any poison ivy. I wish you had warned me."

"If I thought you were going to pick immediately I would have. But I honestly didn't think about it until I was closing down the steam baths."

"Tell me, why do you have to steam the wood?"

Jared went into a description of crafting a wooden-hulled boat—the process of steam-bending the wood, how it enabled the oak to be more pliable, and the research he had done concerning this particular craft's history on the cape.

Alex listened eagerly. "I'm here doing research on my family roots. I've always known about my ancestor being a sea captain and his living on Martha's Vineyard. Since I was small I wanted to come and experience the ocean and the place where my relatives had grown up. Particularly the one who moved to Kansas. . .she had very fond memories of the place."

"So you're a Luce, then?"

"Well, one of his descendants anyway."

"Have you been to the historical society yet?"

"Yesterday I spent the entire day in Edgartown."

"What did you find?"

Alex went over all her discoveries, glad to share them with someone. Finally she mentioned the row of captains' houses with their widows' walks.

Jared broke out in laughter. "Tell me, Doc, do you honestly believe those women had nothing better to do with their time, knowing their husbands were out for years at a stretch?"

"No, I figured they only used them when they knew it was about time for their return."

"Sorry to burst your romantic bubble, but widows' walks were not built for searching for husbands."

"They weren't?"

"No. In fact, they had a far more practical use. They were used to extinguish chimney fires in the winter. If you noticed, the roofs in the area tend to have steep peaks."

"Yes, I noticed that. Why?"

"Because of snow. The steeper a peak, the less likely the snow and ice would build up on your roof. Anyway, if you got a fire in your chimney it was virtually impossible to make it up the roof in the winter. So the more well-to-do families put in these walkways between the chimneys. At the base of each chimney was a bucket of sand to be poured down the flue to extinguish the fire."

"Really?"

He seemed pleased with her interest. "Really. I see we

have something in common. We both love history and, in particular, island history and some of the folklore that surrounds it."

"How did the story of widows' walks ever get started in the first place?"

"I don't know. Probably some writer one time looked at the old sea captains' houses and just assumed. Even though it's not true, it does give quite a romantic side to sailors and their loves, don't you think?"

"I suppose, but wouldn't it make more sense to simply tell everyone the truth?"

"Probably." Jared chuckled. "But fiction is sometimes more interesting."

She smiled. *Strange*, she thought, *how this man can be so charming*. Absentmindedly she scratched her legs.

"Stop that," he bellowed.

Startled, Alex jumped.

"Sorry, I didn't mean to scare you. But you can't scratch. Those abrasions are bad enough. If any of them were made by a poison ivy twig you are going to have a very bad case."

"I know. I forgot."

Jared scraped the chair backward, got up, and grabbed the bottle of calamine lotion. "Come on, let me rub this on you."

"Yes, Doctor," she teased.

"Well, one of us ought to be."

Alex pointed her leg toward him. He squatted in front of her. He poured the lotion onto a couple of cotton balls and dabbed it on her open wounds. His touch was gentle but very methodical. Once he finished one area he moved on to the next. Over and over he repeated the process. Aware she was feeling too much pleasure from his attention, she thanked him and pulled her legs back under her chair.

"You're welcome. Good night, Alexandria. Here's my number if you need anything."

"Thank you, Jared. I'm sure I'll be fine."

"I'm sure you will be too, but just in case."

❧

He slipped out the door slowly. Being so close to her, feeling her skin, sensing her vulnerability, was too much. He wasn't going to allow himself to get that close to the woman again. *Sure, we can be friends, but that's it.*

But whatever he told himself didn't work. He was concerned about her poison ivy reaction, and something almost primal developed in him, a powerful urge to watch over and care for her. It felt natural, instinctive, almost spiritual. *Maybe that's it, God giving me a tender heart to aid the sick.* That must be it. Jared relaxed. He was simply living his Christian life and putting it into action by coming to her rescue and tending to her needs. There was nothing more, just good, common, brotherly love that Christ gives His people for one another.

At peace with this revelation, he settled in for the night. He had his devotions, said his closing prayers for the day, and fell fast asleep. This was the first night since Dr. Alexandria Tucker imposed herself on his life that he actually was going to get a restful sleep.

❧

The next few days went smoothly between Alex and Jared. He continued to check on her. The first couple of days she was quite sick, but there wasn't much he could do for her. It was a simple case of waiting out the poison in her system. After the first night's application of calamine lotion, neither one of them had wanted a repeat performance. She was feeling better now, and the poison ivy was drying up. She felt well enough to continue her research at the historical society.

Each evening she read a couple of chapters of *Lost at Sea*. The story captivated her, not so much because of the terror of the ordeal as because of the author's openness about his fears, anger, and past grievances with God. And yet the man never seemed to gain release from the anguish of losing his loved ones. He at last accepted his loss as God's timing, but he still wouldn't allow his heart to be vulnerable again.

Having taken her evening shower, Alex cinched her bathrobe and wrapped her wet hair in a towel-turban high upon her head.

"Alexandria?" Jared yelled as the door slammed against the inner wall.

Anger, fused by embarrassment, fueled her sharp response. "What on earth are you doing plowing in here again?"

"Sorry, it's important."

"No, Jared, it's not so important that you couldn't have knocked."

His cheeks flushed and his neck turned crimson. "There's a nor'easter coming, possibly turning into a hurricane."

"What?"

"Sorry, I didn't mean to barge in, but I need your help. We need to protect the houses."

Flustered, pushing down her surge of anger, she said in level tones, "I'll get dressed. What can I do?"

"I need you to help hold some plywood in place. We need to board the windows, and especially the sliding glass door."

"I'll be right out." Alex hurried into the bedroom, pulling her robe off as she walked. *What was a northeaster?* she wondered. The fact that it could turn into a hurricane was enough of a warning. She remembered news footage of Hurricane Andrew in Florida a few years back, and various other hurricanes in years since. She knew the potential dangers. "Oh, Lord, protect us. We are on the shore, the first houses to get hit."

Dressed in mere moments, she hurried outside. *There was a steady breeze, but nothing major,* she thought. She ran around the house looking for Jared.

"Jared?" she called. Nothing, no response. She ran down to the boathouse. He wasn't there. She looked down the hill toward Jared's home, which was closer to the shore and lower on the bluff. Seeing him working around the house closing the wooden shutters over the windows, relief washed over her. Something about his presence was reassuring. For the first time in her life she actually saw working wooden shutters. All of her experience had been with decorative ones.

When she joined him at his cottage, he explained how to secure the shutters. She took over that job and he gathered various outdoor items and placed them either under the house or inside it. The items under the house he secured with tarps and rope, tying them to circular concrete columns that obviously supported the building. Once his place was done, they headed up to the Trainers' home; she carried a couple of hammers and a bag of nails while he carried a few sheets of plywood. The wind was gathering its strength, and the plywood he carried became like wooden sails.

"Can I help?"

"No, I've got them thanks."

Mr. Macho probably figures he can handle them easier without my help, she reasoned, foregoing an argument with him about how strong she was.

At the house the first thing Jared boarded up, after placing the deck furniture in the living room, was the sliding glass door that faced the ocean. Under the deck he pulled out pre-cut pieces of plywood with numbers on them. "Alex, that's window number one."

She nodded.

"We start there and work around the house. Each board is cut for each window."

"I understand. Do you want me to nail or to carry the wood?"

"I'll carry and help you set the first couple nails. Then while I'm gathering more boards and securing the outdoor items under the deck you can finish securing each board."

"Fine. Show me the way, captain."

He grinned. Alex smiled and quickly averted her gaze. Instead, she went straight to work. Sprinkles of rain started to fall on her cheeks. She looked to the sky in the direction of the northeast. Sure enough, on the horizon, were intense black clouds.

"Alex, I can finish. I need you to prepare for loss of power. The water is from a well and is pumped by an electric generator, so if we lose power, we lose water. Fill every tub and sink. Go to my place and do the same. Also, at the Trainers' take every pitcher and tall container that can hold water and get us a few gallons for drinking."

"Okay. What else?"

"Locate any candles and flashlights, and turn the refrigerator up to high. Get it really cold. Place some water in large plastic bags with those fancy zipper-type seals into the freezer and make some blocks of ice."

"Sure." Alex knew about preparing for loss of power, having lived through enough windstorms and tornadoes in Kansas. She assumed the same kind of preparations needed there would work here as well.

"After that, run to the store and pick up some nonperishables. If we lose power we could be without it for several days. When I'm done up here, I'm going to the boathouse to secure things down there."

"All right." Alex fought back her desire to challenge his ordering attitude. *He's simply focused*, she told herself. Typical male. She nodded and headed into the house.

❧

Jared placed the last board up on the Trainers' home. Down at the boathouse, he secured the loose planks, tying them together and placing them alongside the walls. The boathouse only had three walls, the fourth was open to the sea.

Jared gathered his tools, loaded his wooden toolbox, and brought the rest to his house. He secured the steam baths that lay along two walls. Having made them himself, he hated the thought they might be lost.

After storing the toolbox inside the cottage, he returned to the boathouse. Rolling up his blueprints, he placed them back inside a cardboard tube. He gathered together additional items to take out of harm's way. Various shades of ominous gray filled the sky, streaked with occasional lightning. He thanked the Lord there was no evidence of circular movement, thus little threat of a hurricane, yet he knew that northeasters could have winds as strong as hurricanes.

Hearing the latest news update in the shop reminded him he needed a battery-operated radio. "I can't forget that." He placed it on his mental to-do list. The ribbed hull of his boat lay like an empty skeleton before him. He winced, knowing it would be hit, hoping it would be spared the pounding of the waves. He sighed. "Oh well, Lord, it's in Your hands. I can always rebuild."

In his cottage, he deposited the items he had gathered from the boathouse. Anything that could become a missile propelled by the wind was now neatly tucked away or tied down. Grabbing his radio, he checked the batteries. They were weak. He searched through his junk drawer for some fresh batteries, grateful to find a few. He also retrieved a camping lantern, which he set aside to be taken up to the Trainers' home. Turning his refrigerator on high, he placed some water jugs in the freezer.

He paused suddenly, realizing he hadn't asked Alex's permission to stay with her through the storm. He rolled his shoulders and stretched his neck, hoping she wouldn't take offense, counting on her being happy with his company through the rough hours of the storm.

The increased wind howled through the shutters. Rain began its gentle drumming on the roof. Scurrying through his cabinets, he grabbed some canned goods and the steak that was thawing on the counter for dinner. He drove his truck to the backside of his house, furthest from the assaulting winds, trusting that the house would help protect it from flying debris.

❧

At the grocery store, some folks were panicking, others taking a more carefree approach, as if it were just another day. Alex picked up sodas, dehydrated and canned juices, fresh vegetables and fruit that would last without refrigeration, canned meats, soups, and canned vegetables. The shelves were sparse, at best, as she went through the aisles. She calculated for three days' supply, since Jared said if they lost power it could possibly take that long for the electric to be restored. With her shopping cart full, she stood in line. Every register was open. Five people stood in front of her waiting their turn with the cashier.

One woman talked serenely about how she'd been through many storms like this and worse. Her words calmed a nervous mother with children.

Alex glanced over her shoulder and saw a mother with a small child standing behind her in line. Her cart was nearly empty, her eyes glistened with tears. Other carts behind her were nearly empty as well. "Excuse me," Alex said, "is that all you could find?"

The woman nodded her head.

"How many children do you have?"

"Four."

"Do you have more nonperishable food at home?"

"No, tonight is grocery night. I couldn't get to the store until my husband came home with his paycheck."

Alex scrutinized the array of food in her own cart. There was far more than two people could eat or needed to eat over three days. "Here, take some of mine." The young mother looked on in wonder. "Please, take what you would like from my cart."

"I can't. It's yours." The woman's eyes looked away from her as she bit her lower lip.

"I merely reached the shelves before you were able to. Please, I really don't need all of this food. I want you to have it."

"Are you sure?" She searched Alex's eyes for affirmation.

"Yes." Alex played with the little girl standing in the cart. She had a headful of blond curls and one of the deepest set of brown eyes Alex had ever seen.

The young mother tentatively reached into Alex's cart. Alex's heart was full, and she knew she had done the right thing. There was no way she could have lived with herself knowing a family of six would possibly go hungry for the next few days.

Gradually the mother's actions became more relaxed. She took most of Alex's purchases. "Are you sure this is all right?"

"Yes, it's only myself and one other. And there's enough food back at the house."

"Thank you, I simply don't know what else to say."

"Thank the Lord, and do something nice to someone else when it comes your time to give and serve."

She nodded. Alex was next. She placed the remaining items on the conveyer belt. She noticed her act of kindness was caught by others in line. People started sharing their acquisitions with other customers around them. *Storms have a way of making you hoard things, or they pull people together*, Alex hypothesized.

The cashier ran her order through the scanner and winked at her when she paid.

"Thanks again," the young mother said as Alex gathered her bags into her arms.

"You're welcome. I'll pray for you and your family to weather the storm safely."

The young mother nodded and concentrated on getting her groceries ready for the cashier.

Confident in having done the right thing, Alex walked with her shoulders straight and her heart full of Christian love.

six

His home secure, Jared worked his way once again up the hill to the Trainers' house. Stopping on the bluff, he stood scanning the horizon. The clouds were gray and deepening to charcoal. The dance of lightning highlighted the clouds and showed their tumultuous drift toward shore.

Memories of a similar storm flickered with bits and pieces of the past. Images of that fateful storm momentarily paralyzed him. He was back on the *Kontiki Too*. Working the rigging, lowering the mainsail, trying to keep the boat pressed into the wind. Waves crashed over the bow; she was taking in some water. He had been fighting the storm for hours, but he continued struggling with the rudder despite the weariness of his body. Fatigued, he held the tiller with what strength he could muster. He had prayed the storm would soon be over, even though the horizon was obliterated by the black, ominous sky.

A forceful gust of wind jarred him back to reality. He squeezed his eyes shut and let out a deep breath. *Today's storm takes precedence; keep yourself in the present, old boy*. With determined strides he marched toward the Trainers' home.

His hands full with the items from his cottage, he tapped the door with his leather workboot. The chill of the wind seeped through his rain-drenched shirt. "Hi. I've brought a few things."

As Alex held the door open for him, he turned sideways

and stepped through. "I've got a lantern here, another flashlight and a few canned goods." He placed the bags on the table. "Also, I was thawing a steak earlier today so I thought we could share it for dinner."

"Planning on camping out?"

Is she upset? He turned and caught the twinkle in her eye. "If you don't mind, I thought I'd spend the worst of the storm here with you rather than on the beach."

"Sounds great. Jared, I didn't get much from the grocery store."

"I hoped you would get there before it was wiped out."

"Well, not exactly. The shelves were pretty sparse, but there was this woman. . ." Alex retold the incident.

"I would have done the same. I'm sure with what you and I have together we'll be fine."

"I'm glad you understand."

"The good Lord wouldn't want it any other way," he smiled.

"Can I ask you another question?"

Her eyes were not quite looking straight at him, and Jared assumed she was nervous, maybe embarrassed to be asking whatever question she possibly had in mind. "Sure."

"Are you a believer? I mean, you know, a born-again Christian?"

"Yes, although I haven't always lived in a manner that was pleasing to the Lord. You are also, aren't you?"

"Yes."

He had known she must be. Aware that they now had two things in common, he believed God was using this woman to strengthen him as a Christian. "I thought so."

"How?"

"Little things said, and the way you prayed over breakfast the day I fixed the hot water heater."

"Oh."

"Well, how about that steak?"

"Sounds great to me. One thing I'm not worried about—with propane tanks for the stove we'll be able to cook."

"You're a wise woman. Let me clean up and I'll give you a hand with dinner."

"Sure, how do you like your steak?"

"Rare, what about you?"

She chuckled. "The same."

さ

The wind whistled as it rushed through the plywood sheets across the slider. Rain pelted the house from all sides. Alex found herself a little disoriented. With all the windows boarded, an eerie feeling seized her, like being shut up within a darkened elevator. "Jared, how long do these northeasters last?"

"The better part of a day, generally, but sometimes they've lasted a couple." Getting up from the table, he turned on the Trainers' stereo. "Let's check on the status of the storm."

Alex listened to the crackle of the static as Jared tried to get a clear fix on the area radio station. Once located, they listened, learning the storm would continue for hours. Most of the island still had power as the more intense part of the storm was just about to hit shore. She thought about the book she had been reading, about its description of the storm, about being on a small boat in the middle of a raging sea. Thankful she was on dry land, she allowed her uneasy feelings to dissipate. "How many of these northeasters have you been through?"

"I suppose we have at least one a year. Although this is early in the season for it."

The power cut out. Jared turned on the flashlight. Alex

grabbed the matches and lit the lantern and a few candles.

Tree limbs snapped around them. Lightning cracked right outside the house. Alex jumped. It sounded so close. Mere milliseconds later she heard the ripping of wood. Thump! The house groaned. Something large had just landed on the roof over the back bedroom.

Before checking out the damage, Jared lifted the phone. "It's dead also. Someplace down the road the phone and power lines must have been knocked out where they merge."

The intensity of the storm escalated. Between the darkness and the loss of power, they were totally at the disposal of the elements. *Relax!* Alex chastised herself.

Jared went back to check on the damage. She sat alone. The howling of the wind, the waves crashing on the beach, the rain, everything seemed crystal clear. She could picture it even though she sat completely blocked from seeing anything outside.

"The ceiling looks fine. I don't know how bad the roof is. We'll have to check periodically for leaking," Jared said, as he walked into the glow of the candlelit room.

Alex blinked at Jared's shadowy hulk. He would be an intimidating man if she didn't know him. "I don't mind telling you this is a little frightening."

"I know, but I've been through worse."

"When, what happened?"

Jared sat down beside her on the couch. "Imagine yourself being out there," he pointed toward the ocean, "on a fairly small vessel in the middle of the sea and a storm of even stronger winds comes up."

"Oh my, what happened?"

She watched him close his eyes. Slowly he opened them. "It was a while ago. I had built a ship to cross the Atlantic.

Actually the goal was to sail around the world eventually, but. . ." He paused for a moment, then continued. "I was seven days out when it started to rain. I grabbed my foul-weather gear and trimmed the sails. A little rain never killed a sailor. The entire first day was light rain with some occasional downpours. The wind picked up as the sun went down. I battened down the boat, rigged up an autopilot of sorts, and went to sleep, hoping the storm would be over by morning."

Alex thought back on the story she had been reading. It was the same technique used by the man who was lost at sea. "What happened?"

"When I got up the next morning the skies were far more threatening. I had sailed smack dab into the heart of the storm. Of course, I didn't know it at the time. I took in the jib, lowered the mainsail some more and headed straight into the wind. The seas were rolling twelve to fifteen feet at this point. It's an awesome sight seeing a wall of ocean water right over your shoulder."

"I think it would be a terrifying sight."

"That, too, but it's amazing how water moves."

"I suppose. What happened next?"

"That went on for hours, with the waves increasing in size. I was getting nowhere. Not that I was really trying to do anything more than stay afloat, of course."

"How small was this boat?"

"The main hull was about sixteen feet."

"What? Are you crazy? You were trying to cross the Atlantic in a sixteen-foot boat?"

Jared grinned. "I was trying to prove a historical point."

Alex laughed. "What was that, that a man is just as ignorant as his forefathers?"

"Now, hang on, Alex. I did a lot of research and I modernized the hull, making it fiberglass and more seaworthy. Plus, it was a tri-hulled vessel."

Her mind was back on the book. That boat was also small, also had three hulls, and had also been caught in a storm. It couldn't be, could it? "Jared, what's your last name?"

"Madeiras, why?"

"I've been reading a book about a man who was lost at sea for eight days, written by a J. Madeiras. I take it, that is you?" *And you've stolen my heart,* she refused to tell him. How could she possibly tell him that she had fallen in love with the man in the book?

"How on earth did you find a copy of that book?"

"Brad and Phyllis have a copy in their library. It's yours, right? You're the same man?"

"Yes."

Compassion seized her heart. She remembered the longing she felt for this man, how he still needed to get over some of his hurts. She wondered if they still remained. "You said in the dedication, it was to your loved ones lost. Who were they?"

"My folks, and. . ."

And who? she wanted to ask.

"Hannah, my fiancée."

Alex reached out and gently touched his forearm. Her fingers tingled from the contact. She pushed the sensation out of her mind. "I'm so sorry, Jared. What happened?"

"If you don't mind, I prefer not to talk about Hannah."

"All right." This was crazy. Every ounce of her being wanted to know what was behind those darkened eyes. Had Hannah run off with someone else? No, it couldn't be that. He said "lost." Hannah must have died. Did he feel responsible in some way? She longed to ask more questions, but the man she was getting to know demanded to no longer be approached on the subject. Not now, not yet. *I've pretty near a whole year to get it out of him, if need be. After all, it's not like I'm willing to tell him about Peter.* Calming herself down, she refused to allow herself to feel slighted by his unwillingness to talk about Hannah.

"Do you understand?" He searched her eyes.

His deep probing made her uncomfortable. "Let's just say I have some things I'm not quite ready to discuss with you either."

"Fair enough."

"So, tell me why the Polynesians? What sparked your interest in them and their vessels?"

Jared went on to explain how he had read a story about the Kontiki in high school, how he researched it and finally built his replica, with some modern-day advances, of course. "Basically it came down to the type of storm, and how strong it was. No one in that size of a boat, or even in some larger vessels, would have made it safely through. It took the rescuers eight days to locate me because I was so far off course."

"I simply can't imagine it. I mean, I read your book and I could picture it, but there's no way I can truly understand the anguish of bobbing up and down on the ocean for eight days with no control."

"It's a humbling experience." His voice sounded contrite.

လ

The storm was abating. Jared looked at his watch. He and Alex had played competitive games of rummy, Scrabble, Monopoly, and now chess. As he tapped the black rook he moved in for the kill. "Check."

He loved how Alex bit her lower lip when she was thinking. She moved her queen into a vulnerable spot.

He took his castle and captured her queen. "Check again."

He watched in astonishment as she moved her knight. "Checkmate," she smirked.

His face fell, even though he tried not to show his amazement at her sneaky victory. He examined the board, looking for a possible move that would get him out of the trap she had laid. Nope, she had him pure and simple. "How did you do that?"

Alex chuckled. "Years of practice."

"With whom?"

"First my father, then when I was on my college chess team."

"You competed?"

"Yes. I suppose you think I should have warned you first."

"It would have been nice, knowing in advance I was headed for a slaughter." She was a complicated woman; he was beginning to discover that.

"Men."

"What's that supposed to mean?" *Maybe not that complicated, if she lumps all men up into one category.*

"Nothing, I suppose, but it seems every man I play just hates to lose to a woman."

"That's a sexist statement if ever I heard one."

"Maybe, but it's held true for me. I watched the guys in competition for years. They had no problem being sacked by a guy but as soon as a woman, or myself in particular, beat them, then they were outraged. Sorriest bunch of losers you ever did see."

"I was not bellyaching about losing to you."

"No, to your defense you took defeat like a man. However, I did see your face fall in shock."

"I was shocked by the move, not that you are a woman."

She seemed to ponder this for a moment. "I take it back. You're one rather unique man."

Jared twisted a smile. "Thanks, I think."

"Trust me, it's a compliment. What time is it?"

"A little past midnight. Getting tired?"

"Yes."

"I'm going to go outside and inspect the damage. If you want I'll go to my cabin right afterward, then you can rest."

"Do you think the worst is past?"

"Yes. Do you need me to stay?"

"No, I'll be fine. Thanks for offering, though. Please stop back in and let me know what you find before you go back to your place."

"No problem." He hesitated, realizing he had been hoping they would talk more. He had wanted to share about Hannah as the evening wore on. There was something about Alex that compelled him to open himself up. *But it would be foolish to say something after making such a fuss about not saying anything,* he reasoned.

He got up and took the large flashlight with him. "I'll be back in a few."

As he stepped out the door, he held the screen door tight. The force of the wind was still something to contend with. He worked his way around the back of the house, stepping over downed limbs. The beam of light showed the debris scattered across the path to the back of the house. A large pine tree lay across the back corner of the roof.

There was damage. He decided the ceiling would probably need repairing after the water seeped its way in. The damage to the house was just as Jared expected.

The wind howled through the trees; the rain stung his cheeks. He fought his way around the corner of the house, walking into the wind. The oak and maple leaves made the ground slick. He turned and examined this angle of the house. Dimly the flashlight showed the fallen tree, a gaping hole of broken wood and missing shingles. Obviously, as the storm continued to blow, it continued to damage the weakened roof. Jared tried to step up on a log and get a better angle, but the wind was too strong. His footing slipped and he fell to the ground.

The storm was picking up again. Getting himself up off the ground, he turned toward the shore. It was still too dark, so there was nothing to see. No stars, no moon, only dark clouds surrounded him. Rather than go back the way he came, he decided to cross the front of the house and see how the deck was faring.

As he turned the corner, he received the full impact of the wind. Pressing each step deeper into the ground, he worked his way to the stairs. The deck was covered with debris, broken limbs, pieces of trash.

Crack! Jared turned just in time to see a limb propelling itself toward him. He tried to duck. He went down. Darkness enveloped him. His mind flashed back to another dark time, his lungs burning under the water, constricting from lack of air.

&

Alex paced. Jared should be back by now. *Where is he? Why hasn't he come back?* She looked at her watch and realized he'd been gone for half an hour. *Something's not right.* Alex ran to her closet, grabbed a raincoat, and took the other flashlight.

The screen door wrenched out of her hands as the wind caught it. Grunting, she wrestled it closed. The wind pushed her quickly off the back of the deck and around to the rear of the house. Swinging the flashlight from side to side, she probed the darkness. No Jared.

"Jared!" she yelled. "Jared!" But no response. She forged her way to the back corner of the house where the tree had come down. As she rounded the corner she called again.

"Jared!"

Concern merged with apprehension as she bent low and leaned headlong into the wind. Bits of sand stung her face. Reaching the front corner of the house, she wondered if maybe he had simply headed back to his place. But she was positive he'd said he would return.

Uncertain what to do, she stood frozen with trepidation. Maybe he'd walked around to the front of the house while she walked around the rear. She maneuvered herself against the wind.

As the beam of light fell on the steps, she saw him collapsed with a limb near his head. "Jared!" She ran to him. Her heart slammed in her chest with fear. "Oh, Lord, let him be all right."

seven

Her fingers worked through his thick locks, feeling for a wound. She knew he was bleeding; she didn't need to turn the flashlight on to see it. Over the years she had felt enough blood. Tenderly she worked her fingers around the wound, testing to see how bad it was. "Jared, can you hear me?"

Knowing he was unconscious, she needed to talk to see if she could help bring him to. "Dr. Tucker" came alive. She kept talking, telling him each and every thing she was doing, checking his pulse, his breathing. He was stable. She lifted his arm across her back and placed her right shoulder under his left armpit. "Come on, Jared, help me here. Ugh, you're built like an ox."

Alex was stronger than most women her size and proper training in emergency rescue gave her the expertise to lift an adult body. But Jared was solid muscle. She was going to need all her strength and concentration to walk him back.

"Come on Jared, wake up. I need some help here."

She raised his body up slightly.

"Lord, help me. Wake this man up."

"Jared, we're going back to the house now. Step forward with your right leg."

Jared mumbled, and his leg moved forward. He wasn't fully conscious, but it was enough.

"Great, now the left. Super, Jared. Come on, a few more steps. Perfect, you're doing perfect. Stay with me, Jared." She was thankful they were only twenty feet from the door. "Don't

73

fall back to sleep. Come on, fight it. That's it, great."

Alex unlatched the screen door and the wind caught it. She was grateful they had been walking with the wind, not against it. She opened the interior door and helped Jared through. "Let's go to the couch, Jared. That's it, a few more steps. You're doing wonderful."

She eased him down on the couch. He was waking, though still groggy. The wound needed to be cleansed and a thorough exam of his injuries needed to be assessed. In her bedroom Alex retrieved her black bag: It was always accessible whether on vacation or a simple errand to the mall. Of course, she left it in her car most of the time, but it was amazing how often she had used it.

She worked quickly and efficiently. Two years of ER training had been a wonderful teacher, not to mention the numerous cuts and spills her regular patients had taken over the years.

"Ow, that stings!"

"Glad to have you back among the living. What happened?"

"Other than a huge hunk of tree plowing into my head, not much."

"Have you ever heard of ducking?"

"I did. It would have landed on my chest if I hadn't."

"Well at least this way it hit a nonvital organ," she teased.

"Anyone ever tell you, you have a lousy bedside manner, Doc?"

"Nope, you're the first one. Now hush for a moment while I stitch up the last couple of sutures."

"Yes, ma'am."

"It's not too bad, Jared. Although we should probably have it x-rayed to be sure."

"Is that really necessary? Can it wait until morning? Personally I'm not up for a drive."

"Yes, it can wait, unless you start showing some other signs—then there's no argument, okay?"

"Fine. Doc, do you mind if I spend what is left of the night on your couch? I don't quite have the stomach to walk to the cottage."

"Are you nauseated?"

"No, not really."

"I'll want to spend the night watching you anyway. You can stay here. How about the guest bed, though, instead of the couch?"

"I wouldn't want to put you out."

Alex laughed. "You've got me performing medical aid with no electric lights, nothing of modern medicine, and you don't want to put me out."

"Well, that's all in the line of the Hippocratic oath isn't it?"

"Jared, you can be such a stubborn. . ."

"So can you, Doc, so can you. How did you get me in here?"

"I'm stronger than I look."

"Yeah, right. You're one pretty skinny little thing."

"Thank you, I think." She was thankful the lights were dim so he wouldn't see her blush. She realized he had sized her up, even as she had noticed him. "You stay down while I make up the bed with fresh linens." Not waiting for a response, she hurried off to one of the other bedrooms, stopping by the linen closet along the way.

❧

Jared's head throbbed with pain. He reached behind and felt the swollen bald spot.

"Try not to touch it."

"Alex?"

"I'm here, Jared."

"Have you been up all night?" He raised his head to look at her.

"I slept some. How are you feeling?"

"Like I got hit by a Mac truck."

"Good."

"Easy for you to say."

She smiled. Jared's heart leaped.

"How's your vision?" Her eyes probed his.

Jared scanned the room. "Fine. Everything is crystal clear."

"Great." Alex held a flashlight in her hand. "Can I look at the wound?"

Rolling to his side, he gave her a better view of his injury. "How's it look?"

"In this light, pretty good. I don't see much infection. I cleansed it a couple of times hoping to get all the bits of bark and debris out."

"Thanks. It's kind of nice having a doctor so close."

Alex chuckled. "You won't think so when you get my bill."

"Hmm, then I withdraw the comment and reserve the right to alter it after I see the bill." Her eyes sparkled with mirth. He took her hand. "Thanks, Alex. I really appreciate your help." He stroked the back of her hand with his thumb. Her silken skin was soft and smooth, so unlike his own hard callused hands.

"You're welcome, but I'm sure you would have done the same for me."

"I would have helped you, but I'm not a doctor. I'm not sure what I would have done with a head wound." He tried to sit up. Dizzy, he grabbed the sides of the bed.

"Hang on there, big fella, you can't move that quickly. You'll black out."

"Now you tell me."

"I didn't know you were going to try and get up."

"You're right. Okay, Doc, what do I need to know?"

"Tell me if you're nauseous, if your vision blurs, or anything that is different than normal."

"I can do that. Can I walk?"

"Yes, but slowly. It was a fairly deep wound and you lost a bit of blood. You'll live, though."

"Thanks, I think." Jared rubbed the back of his neck. "I don't hear the storm. Has it stopped?"

"Finally."

"Can I go outside and inspect?"

"Only if I can tag along." Alex stood with her hands on her hips.

Man, she's a beautiful woman. "Okay."

"Need a hand?"

She held her hand out to him. He didn't think he really needed it but the memory of how her hand felt in his encouraged him to grasp it anyway. "Thanks."

"You're welcome. Now take it slow. You'll be feeling better in a few more hours, unless there's something more going on up there."

"Like what?"

"Oh, a cracked skull for instance." She winked.

☙

The walk around the house exhausted Jared. Alex wondered if she had allowed him to do too much too soon. "Jared, I want to take you to the hospital and have your skull x-rayed."

"Is it really necessary? I feel fine, just tired."

"I thought we went through this last night. It's just a precaution, but one I would really like to have done."

"All right, I'll be a good patient. But we'll need to take a chain saw with us. There might be downed limbs in the road and I'll need to clear a path for us to get out."

"You can't do that kind of work yet."

"Then we sit here."

"Let me try getting out the driveway first, then I'll come back and get you. If we can pass, fine. If I can't move the limbs, then we are sitting right here." There was no way she was going to allow him to exert himself and get that wound bleeding again. Not yet, it was too soon. He needed a day of rest.

"I don't need to sit down. I'm fine."

"Jared, are you going to be a difficult patient or are you going to listen to me?"

"You're a pediatrician, right?"

"Yes."

"Well, kids may need a rest but a man doesn't."

Alex laughed so hard she bent over grabbing her sides. "Men, my dear Jared, are the biggest kids of all. You'll take my advice or I'll strap you down in that chair."

"You and what army?"

"I don't need an army. Remember, I got you into the house by myself, didn't I?"

He looked at her, knitting his eyebrows. His gaze scrutinized her arms and legs, trying to assess her strength.

"I'm stronger than I look."

"Apparently."

"Will you behave and stay put while I check on the road?"

"Yes, Doctor."

"Thanks. I don't want to come back and see you've fallen and undone my fancy embroidery."

Jared laughed a deep, barrel-chested laugh. Alex loved the sound, so warm and comforting. *Watch yourself, Alex, you're going to fall for this man if you're not careful.* "I'll be back as soon as possible."

"Be cautious, okay?" Jared grabbed her hand.

His touch was electric. She squeezed his hand, trying to counter the emotional charge he was giving her. "I will." Pulling away, she mentally switched gears; she needed to get him to the hospital.

She blinked her eyes against the bright sun. The sky was a rich blue, laced with fleeting, pure white clouds. At the sight of her Bronco, a sick feeling washed over her. Something had smashed her rear window. She examined the car more closely. A chunk of brick, about the size of her palm, lay on the back seat. The bits of glass seemed to be contained to the rear of the car. But as a precaution, she ran her hands across the driver's seat. The thought of sitting on a piece of glass was painful enough, but the prospect of having it extracted even more embarrassing. The seat was clear. She made a mental note to check the other one before Jared sat in it.

The long drive out to the main road was littered with small branches and tons of leaves. Slowly, she worked her way through the debris. Occasionally, some larger limbs blocked her path. Each time she encountered one, she would get out and move it over to the side.

A large tree with a trunk nearly a foot in diameter lay completely across the dirt road. Spotting a house through the trees, she turned off the Bronco and headed through the woods. She found a middle-aged man working in his yard. "Excuse me. I'm Dr. Tucker. I'm staying in the Trainers' home this winter. I need some help. There's a fallen tree in the road and I need to get Jared Madeiras to the hospital."

"Is Jared okay? How bad is he?"

"He's fine, I think. He was hit in the head by a tree limb last night. I've treated the wound, but I would like to have x-rays done."

"Let me grab my chain saw and my boys. We'll have the tree moved in a few minutes. Where is it?"

Alex turned and pointed to her Bronco. "Just in front of my car."

"Okay, the rest of the road is clear. We'll take care of that, you go back and get Jared. Hopefully by the time you get back we'll have enough of it clear for you to pass."

"Thanks, I really appreciate this."

"No problem. Anything for Jared."

Alex smiled. She wondered if that meant if someone else were injured he wouldn't be so quick to help, but she tossed the thought aside. From her experience so far, these islanders didn't have a problem lending a hand.

Back at the house she found Jared asleep in the chair. His face, even with its day-old stubble, stirred in her a longing to reach out and caress him. Resisting the urge, she simply placed her hand on his shoulders. "Jared, the road is clear."

He snapped his eyes open. The corners of his lids crinkled in the hint of a smile. Her palm suddenly warmed, and she pulled it off of his strong muscular frame as if it would catch on fire.

"Okay. There weren't any branches in the road?"

"A few. The smaller ones I moved. Some of the neighbors are removing a tree."

"Which neighbors?"

"I'm not sure. I didn't get their names."

"Doesn't matter, I'll find out later."

"Let's get that head of yours examined." *And maybe my own. Goodness, I'm falling for this man, and fast.*

❧

Jared nodded in and out during the trip to the hospital. He was fine, he knew he was, just tired and weak. He figured it was due to the amount of blood he lost. Somehow, he wasn't quite sure how, Alex had him change his shirt, or maybe she had done it. That reminded him of her hands on his shoulders moments before they left the house, waking him with the searing awareness of her touch. He needed to guard himself. She was too captivating. He was falling for this woman.

The hospital was in chaos, so many people, so many needs. He watched as Alex gave a hand helping with the emergency patients. He marveled at her care and compassion, and her professionalism, all embodied in a delicate female frame. Rolling his eyes away from Alex, he realized he needed to get his mind off of her. Moment by moment, movement by movement, she was drawing him into her web. *I won't do it. I'll not allow another in. Too much heartache, I can't go through that again, Lord. Help me keep her at bay.*

Two hours went by before his x-rays. He wondered if it would show what was wrong with his thinking, letting a woman get under his skin. How could he open his heart to a woman, to anyone? The mere thought made him nervous. She was his neighbor. That made for further complications. They would be seeing each other on a daily basis. Panic infused his body. His torso stiffened. *How on earth am I going to keep from falling in love with her?* Every time he caught a glimpse of her, he was drawn into her snare. With a hopeless sigh, he tossed down the magazine he had been trying to read. *Oh, Lord, give me strength. I'm not sure I can endure this test. The woman sets my mind a-buzzing. I need help here, Lord.*

After the x-rays, which showed no internal bleeding and no fractures, he was ready to go home. But Alex wasn't. She was needed here. He loved how she worked. So careful and tender with her hands. She really did have a wonderful bedside manner, especially with the children, helping them, calming them down. She was a natural. "Alex, can I drive home? I'll come back and get you. There's nothing I can do here."

"Actually there is, Jared, if you want to lend a hand."

"What can I do? I'm no doctor."

"Let me show you." Alex led him to the entrance. "See all these people? They need to be registered and signed in. As you can see, the folks here are working their fastest, but the hospital is packed."

Jared nodded, not quite sure what she was getting at. She knocked on the window of one of the registrars. "Excuse me, I've got a volunteer here who is willing to lend a hand with light stuff. He has a head wound, so no lifting, okay?"

The woman was surprised, but she accepted the doctor's offer.

"She'll tell you what to do," Alex told Jared. "I'll be in the ER."

"Okay. Alex, you're. . ." He cut himself off; what was he going to tell her? She's a great doctor? Or her heart was so tender and loving to people?

Jared worked for several hours until weariness overtook him. He stretched and rubbed the back of his neck, figuring if he was tired Alex must be also. The number of new patients coming in had dropped considerably in the past hour. "Melissa, I'm going to find Dr. Tucker and take her home. The woman has been up all night taking care of me, and now she's worked almost another six hours straight in the ER."

"Sounds good, Jared. Thanks for your help."

"You're welcome, no problem."

Jared searched the ER and found Alex leaning against a wall with her eyes closed. "Alex?"

"Jared. How are you feeling?" She stood erect and appeared to be ready to go back to work.

"Fine, but you're exhausted. I'm taking you home."

"I really should stay and help."

Her shoulders slumped. She was tired and he knew it. "No, you've been helping enough. Now you're exhausted, so you are going home. That's an order, Doc."

"Aye-aye, Captain," she said with a mock salute.

Alex said her good-byes and the staff thanked her for her help. The hospital administrator gushed over her so with his appreciation that Jared eyed him suspiciously. Was he hitting on her? Alex offered her phone number, informing him how long she would be in the area, and suggesting that if they found themselves short sometime to give her a call.

"I'm driving," Jared insisted as they walked through the parking lot.

Alex tossed him the keys. "Sounds like the Jared I know. You must be feeling better."

"Must be." There was no way he was going to tell her how protective he felt of her. He knew she must be dead on her feet.

As he drove up the island, she fell asleep almost immediately. He watched the tension ebb from her body. She was an altogether desirable woman. The rest of the trip he glued his eyes to the road. Refusing to look at her was the only safe way to keep his thoughts in check.

"Wake up, Alex, we're home."

eight

The annoying sound of an engine made Alex cringe under the covers. Sunlight poured through the window. "Sunlight?" She strained through closed lids at the window. The plywood had been removed. *When did Jared take them off?* she wondered. Moaning, her feet hit the floor. The irritating noise outside continued to grate on her nerves. "Why can't the man simply wait until someone is up and awake?" she mumbled, heading into the bathroom.

A shower, a nice hot shower. Her mumbling turned to a whine. The tub was still full of water. There was no power, there would be no shower. She boiled some water and proceeded with a sponge bath. "Dear, Lord, thank You that I was born in the twentieth century. Would You mind terribly hurrying along those repairmen?"

After dressing, she noticed every window was unboarded. Certain it was Jared making that irritating noise, she went outside to track down the source of her discontent.

Turning off the chain saw, he called out to her. "Hi! Sleep well?"

"Until a few minutes ago. What on earth are you doing making all that racket?"

"I'm cleaning up after the storm. Sorry I woke you, but it is noon."

"Noon? Don't tell me I slept the morning away."

"Yup. Alex, I need to take care of this tree in order to repair the Trainers' roof."

"Of course. Did you have breakfast?"

"Yes. But some lunch would hit the spot."

"Give me fifteen minutes, I'll fix something, okay? By the way, how's the head?"

"Fine. I'll be in shortly." Jared yanked the pull rope and the chain saw engine sputtered back to life, settling into a low droning sound when he placed it on a log. Somehow it wasn't as annoying now that she knew what he was doing.

Alex marveled she had slept so long, and remembered the sleepless night before. She had worked on adrenaline at the hospital until Jared had insisted, thankfully, on taking her home.

Lunch was a simple fare—some thick, chunky soup, bread and butter, instant orange juice—calculated for Jared's hearty appetite, she hoped.

He knocked and came through the door. Maybe the man would never learn to just wait. On the other hand, it didn't bother her like before. She knew him, trusted him, and certainly wasn't afraid of him. He washed up in the bathroom and joined her at the table.

Linking their hands in prayer, Jared thanked God for His protection and their many blessings.

"How's your boat?" Alex asked, stirring her soup to cool it.

"Considering the storm, not too bad. There are some boards that will need to be replaced. Some sanding too. The wind really pelted the stern—it's pitted in places."

"Can I help?"

"Sure, I never turn down an extra set of hands."

"What about the roof?"

"The damage up there is pretty superficial, but if you wouldn't mind being a gopher, it would speed up the process."

"A gopher?"

Jared grinned. "Yeah, go for this, go for that."

"I'm probably the only gopher with an MD."

"I like educated gophers," he smirked.

"You're bad." Her heart warmed.

"Seriously, though, you could save me time, especially if I don't have to go up and down the ladder so often."

"I don't mind lending a hand. Besides, growing up on the farm teaches you a lot about humility."

"How's that?" Jared sopped up the last of his soup with his bread.

"Well, nothing like taking care of manure to put you in your own place." *Maybe I shouldn't have mentioned manure at the dinner table,* she worried. At home it was easy to have this kind of table discussion, but would Jared take offense to it?

"Suppose so. So you grew up on a farm?"

Alex released her breath, unaware she had been holding it in. "I thought I told you."

"Nope, learning something new about you every day." Jared got up from the table and carried his bowl and cup to the sink.

Alex followed, discussing growing up on a farm, what it was like to get up with the chickens and feed the animals before you fed yourself.

Jared's work on the roof went quickly with her passing along the items he needed. She found she liked being his gopher. There was something special about helping him.

❧

He ripped off the last of the broken shingles. Until they had power he couldn't cut out the damaged section in the plywood. Well, he could, but he didn't want to take all day doing it. *Tomorrow the power should be back on,* he reasoned.

"Alex, hand me that tarp."

"Sure."

She hadn't complained once. The woman was not ashamed of hard work, not at the hospital and not here working beside him. She never let up, but worked diligently.

"That should hold until we have power. You still up for helping with the boat?"

"Sure."

"Great," Jared said, stepping off the ladder.

The woman was nothing less than amazing. More than her beauty was playing havoc with his senses now; her inner beauty, who she was as a person, was so different from his first impressions. Not that he blamed her any longer for being upset that a man, a stranger, had barged in on her. *That was enough to unnerve anyone,* he supposed.

His stomach knotted as the image of his weather-beaten ship stood before him. True, he had seen it last night after they returned from the hospital, but in the light of day. . . He sighed.

Alexandria placed her hand on his forearm. "You can rebuild, Jared, and I'll help you."

"I know, but it's hard when you've given so much of your time and effort and have to regroup and try again."

"I understand. I had a case once where the child was extremely sick. She would start to gain ground, then would fall back and we would try other meds, other treatments, repeating the process. I tested that poor child for everything. I even sent my notes to some of the best specialists. In the end it was simply a case of waiting it out and much, much prayer. God, after all, is still the great physician."

"Let's hope we don't have another storm this season. I'd hate to have to repeat the process again."

The music of her laughter, the warmth of her hand, eased

the loss of his hard work.

"Where do we begin?" she asked timidly.

Taking in a deep breath and letting it out slowly, he walked toward the battered hull. "First we need to clean out the boathouse and get rid of all this sand and debris."

They worked for hours sweeping, shoveling, removing everything under the sun that didn't belong. They worked up a sweat.

"Are you thirsty?" she asked.

"Parched!"

"How about if I run up to the house and bring us something to drink?"

"Sounds like a plan. If we still have a two-liter of soda, bring a bottle down."

"Sure."

As Alex left, Jared ran to his cottage to gather his tools. It was time to rip off the broken boards. Since the power was still out, he left the power tools in the house. He returned to the boathouse and pulled out his crow bar, a cat's paw, and a hammer. Taking the crowbar, he worked to pull a plank off the ribs he had adhered it to. Several planks had been split due to flying debris.

"Here ya go, Jared, I even chipped some ice for the drinks."

"Great, thanks."

They sat outside the boat house sipping their cold drinks.

"What's that?" Alex pointed toward the ocean.

Jared followed her finger to a boxed crate on the shore.

"That, my dear, may be tonight's supper. Let's go see."

"What is it?"

"It's a lobster pot." Sure enough, there was one good size lobster in it. "Do you like lobster?"

"Yes, but I wouldn't have a clue how to cook it."

"I'll cook the lobster, you can handle the rest of the dinner."

"Sounds fine with me. Tell me how this works."

He knelt down beside the lobster trap. "See the netting on this end?"

Alex nodded.

"Well, lobsters can swim. They swim through this opening which you see gets narrower deeper inside the pot. The bait is tied down here, in the center of the pot. . .see that spike?"

She nodded again, her eyes wide with interest. *The woman has an incredible appetite for knowledge*, he thought.

"Now you see this second net. Well, as the lobster feeds on the bait, it will work its body around and make its way backwards into the opening of the second net. Then it falls into the area where you see the lobster is now."

"Why don't they just swim out?"

"Sometimes they do, but most of the time their big claws are hard to maneuver. Lobsters walk and feed on the ocean floor. Like crabs, they are scavengers."

"So how do these traps stay on the bottom—I mean wood floats, right?"

"Yes. Take a look at the center of the trap where the bait is tied down. That's a concrete ballast. It's enough weight to keep a pot on the bottom, most of the time. Once in a while a storm like the one we had moves them."

"So those buoys in the water are all lobster pots?" Alex pointed to the various small buoys bobbing up and down on the surface of the water.

"Right. Each lobsterman is assigned colors and he paints his buoys accordingly."

"It seems like it would be very easy to steal someone's lobsters. I don't see any kind of police on the water."

"The coast guard are the 'police;' however, most men look

out for each other. Sort of a code of honor. Say, Joe is fishing his pots and sees a stranger fishing others. He'll report it. Most have radios on their boats but for the few that don't, they'll memorize the numbers and get as good a description of the poacher as possible."

"But I hardly see anyone out here."

"True, most guys only come once, maybe twice a week to check their pots. It takes a while to lure the lobsters into the pot."

"This is so interesting. You said you're building your cat-boat to do some fishing with it. Are you planning on doing some lobstering?"

"Yes. You can't stick with one kind of fishing unless you are a deep sea fishermen. Which I don't intend to do."

"I see."

"I need to get back to work, Alex. You don't have to; you've already helped a lot."

"No, I'll help. What do we do with the lobster?"

"Leave him in the pot. If the owner comes by today, it's his. If not, we'll have it for dinner."

"But isn't it stealing?"

"Maybe, except that is Stan's pot. He's a friend, and I'll be telling him about the pot being washed on shore and the lobster we took from it. If he wants to be reimbursed, I'll pay him for it. Although I doubt it. We grew up together."

"It seems to me most islanders know each other."

"The locals tend to. But there are quite a few folks down-island I don't know. I mean, I might know their families somewhere along the line, but not them personally."

"Well, it is a small place."

"Yup. Shall we?"

Alex marveled at the lobster pot. How ingenious. She

wondered who developed the trap. She turned to the ribbed hull of the catboat Jared was building, noticing the pitting the sand had done to the stern; the planks had been cracked from the storm. She longed to help but was no carpenter. Cleaning was the easy part, but to do much more she didn't think was possible for her. "What can I do now Jared?"

"Let's get the baths up and running."

"How are they fueled?"

"Propane. Let me check the lines before I fire them up. I haven't smelled any gas, have you?"

"No."

She watch Jared lie down on the ground, reaching under the long wooden pots he called baths. She had already learned from him that the steaming actually sped up the process of soaking the wood so it could be shaped. He worked his way to the end and repeated the process on the other bath. He followed the lines to the back wall and headed back to the opening. "Where are you going?" she asked him.

"The tanks are on the back of the building. I need to check the connections, plus turn on the tanks. I turned them off for the storm."

"Oh." Embarrassed, she chastised herself. *Why did I have an uneasiness about him leaving my side? Why did I try to get back here so quickly with the drinks? Why do I like just being in this man's presence? This is not good. This is how mistakes are made.*

Jared came back around into the boathouse. His body, his strength, and his mind were all the things Alex had hoped for in a man. But wasn't she here to learn to adjust to never having a man in her life? To accept God's will for the single life? She forced her eyes toward the floor, closed them, and prayed, *Oh Lord, give me strength.*

"Are you okay, Alex?"

She swallowed. "Yes."

"You sure?"

"I'm fine, Jared. Tell me what to do."

"Well, while I'm soaking up some boards we could be sanding some of the rough spots caused by the sand."

"Okay, where's the sandpaper?"

Jared walked to his workbench and opened a drawer, pulling out some sheets. "Here, you can start with this." He ripped the paper in two and folded each half into thirds, giving her a small rectangle of paper to work with. After Jared pointed out where and how she should sand, she went straight to work.

Jared fired up the baths and placed a couple of planks in each tank. He grabbed the other piece of sandpaper and started sanding also.

They worked with no words spoken between them. Alex fought to concentrate on the sanding, but all she could do was think about Jared, about the strength in his fingers, about the gentleness he managed to get out of such powerful hands.

"Ouch."

"What's the matter?"

"My eye, I think I got sawdust in it."

"Let me see."

He wiped his hands on his jeans and cupped her face. She wanted to melt into his arms.

"Close your eyes gently, not tight."

Alex obeyed.

Jared's warm breath flowed over her eyelids as he blew gently. *What on earth is he doing? Driving me crazy, that's what. No, he's just removing the dust. Nothing more. Calm down Alex, you are on sensory overload here.*

"Which eye?"

"My right."

He eased the lid open. She kept the other eye closed. She couldn't bear seeing him up close like this. They were too close; she was too captivated. He was too near; she was too attracted.

"Alex, has anyone ever told you what beautiful eyes you have?"

Oh no. She couldn't afford to hear this, not now, not when she was so vulnerable, when she was about to lose all her self control. "No."

"They're as blue as the Caribbean, glistening in the sun."

Alex opened her eyes now. Jared's fingers caressed her face, his thumbs working their way to her lips. Gaining her voice, she spoke, "Your eyes are darker than mine, more like the Atlantic behind us."

As his eyes searched hers, her body tingled. He was going to kiss her—or was she going to kiss him? It didn't matter; they both moved toward each other. All the passion and pent-up desires from days of longing were caught in the sweetness of his embrace. His lips were soft and tender, sweet as honeycomb.

nine

"Com Electric says just about everyone's power has been restored on the cape and islands after the nor'easter. . ."

The blast of the radio startled Alex as it unexpectedly surged to life. Jared pulled away and Alex jumped back. It wasn't just the radio that frightened her. His kiss burned on her lips. Never had she responded to a man before in that way. Heat rose in her cheeks as she searched for something to focus on, anything but Jared. Why had she kissed him? Why had he kissed her? It was a mistake, a definite mistake. She would never let that happen again.

Jared left her side in haste, as if lightning was about to strike. He turned off the radio; the silence between them was deafening. How could she have let physical desires control her so? Alex's stomach knotted.

"Alex."

She turned.

"I–I. . ."

"I'm sorry too, Jared. It won't happen again. I think I better check the house and see what was left on when the power went out."

"Sure. But we need to talk."

"Later." She couldn't deal with her own feelings now, how could she possibly deal with his? What were his feelings? Why had he kissed her? Could he possibly be attracted to her? Dazed, she walked up the hill.

The house was well-lit, the stereo tuned to the same news

station as outside. Relief washed over her as she heard the newscaster report that no deaths were caused by the storm. She hadn't realized how much concern she felt over the elderly gentleman she had worked on at the hospital the day before. Granted, she only stabilized him, the surgeons were the heroes, but she was glad to know he had made it through the night. The old man's neighbors had brought him in and informed his family. She was falling in love with this place and its people, she realized. She liked being in a small community.

She liked it here, yes, but it was tempting too. Maybe she had never had to deal with temptation before because she was always busy, busy with work, busy with school, busy with chores. When had she even had a chance to fall for someone? Maybe this sabbatical wasn't such a good idea after all. Maybe this sabbatical was the very thing that was wrong with trying to understand God's obvious plan for her life. After all, she was running away from her life, her real life, just by being here.

Besides, as long as she was here, Jared would be too real, too present. Every day she would see him. Every day she would be confronted with temptation. This was not good. Maybe she should pack it up and move back to Kansas. She had already found out so much about her distant relatives and their lives on the Vineyard in the 1800s. It wasn't like she had to stay.

Confused and exhausted, she sat down in a chair and attempted to pray. "Oh, Father God, what just happened? Why am I so attracted to this man? How can I survive this test?" She reached for her Bible and searched the Scriptures, praying, asking for God to show her answers to her many questions. She read about lust, she read about marriage, she read about death, and about an incredible battle in the Old Testament. Praying and reading, she searched for answers, but nothing came. She was still as lost and confused as when she sat down to pray.

"A hot shower, I can finally have a hot shower!" Alex got up and hurried to the bathroom, turned on the tap, and stripped off her clothes so fast, as if it had been a year since her last shower. Stepping into the steaming stream, she tilted her head back. The warm water poured over her chestnut-brown hair, and she sighed with content over the delicious pleasure. She cleansed her hair of the grease and oils of several days, working a rich lather of shampoo soothingly with her fingers. Massaging her scalp, she rinsed the suds from her hair as Jared's kiss flooded back to mind.

"Oh dear." Alex turned the hot water off and stood under the stream of now cold water.

❧

Jared pounded his fist to the hull. "Why did I kiss her?" She obviously wanted to be kissed. *Maybe that was it, she was tempting me.* No, he knew better than that. Alex had been plaguing his mind since she arrived. The woman was the only one to break through the past, to get beyond the memory of Hannah. He shouldn't have kissed her, he knew better. *I'm never getting married. I promised myself I'd never do that.*

Why did I promise that? "Because you don't want to feel the pain of another loss," he argued with himself.

We don't know each other, so why that kiss? She's made it clear she's not interested—or has she? The way she stares at me when she thinks I'm not looking, a man would have to be blind not to notice. But why does it feel so good to have her look at me that way?

Jared walked to his cottage. He needed to talk to her. He had wanted to talk immediately, not that he knew what to say, but she left. What was he going to say, though? *Gee, Alex, sorry about the kiss, you're just too enchanting! Oh, I got it, "too beguiling."* No that wouldn't work. Jared raked his fingers through his hair. The sawdust, dirt, and grime from the past few days had taken their toll. Time for a shower.

His shower was both relaxing and unnerving at the same time. He couldn't shake his need to talk to her.

He slammed his hand to his forehead: the lobster! He rushed down the shore, pulled the pot out of the water, and retrieved the shellfish. "You, sir," he said, holding it up in the air, "are my peace offering."

With lobster in hand, he gained ground in seconds. His large bold strides worked their way up the hill and onto her deck. His knock was timid at first, the second, bolder.

He studied his shoes. *What am I going to say?*

"Jared."

He held the lobster up. "The three of us had a date."

Her cheeks flamed.

"Alex, we need to talk, please let me in."

She stepped aside. He walked passed her, ever so careful that their bodies not touch.

"First, let's make dinner. We can talk while we eat."

"Okay."

Jared wasn't comfortable with the cat and mouse game they played with each other during the dinner preparations, but he wasn't ready to broach the subject of their kiss any more than Alex was.

"The lobster smells great." Alex leaned over the red, fully steamed lobster.

"Can't forget the butter." A step and a half later Jared was at the stove grabbing the small pan he had melted butter in.

He poured it into a small clear custard dish and placed it on the table.

Alex had made some potatoes au gratin and cooked up several frozen vegetables, since they had partially thawed during the power shortage.

When they had sat down at the table, Jared didn't attempt to take Alex's hand for the prayer. Instead they clasped their own hands and bowed their heads. "Father, thank You for Your bounty and we ask that You bless this food to our bodies. In Jesus' name, Amen." *And, Lord, bless our conversation also*, he added silently.

He broke up the lobster, dividing it equally. She passed him some potatoes. He took a smaller portion than usual. Was he going to be able to eat? His throat felt constricted.

"Alex, I'm sorry I was so forward today," he breathed. *That wasn't so bad now, was it? Nope, heart surgery would have been easier.*

Her eyes assaulted him. "We were both guilty."

"Maybe so, but I'm the man, I'm responsible."

"It's the nineties, Jared, equal pay for equal work. In other words, we are equally responsible for our own actions."

"Alex, don't take this wrong, but I don't want to get involved."

"Neither do I."

"What?" *Why wouldn't she want to get involved with me?* Never had he imagined that someone wouldn't want to. All the women before he had to fight off with a stick. Well, maybe not a stick, but still, this was different. It wasn't vanity. At least he didn't think it was. He was a fairly attractive man, or so he had been led to believe.

"Jared." She placed her fork on her plate and clasped her hands. "I came here to sort out my life. I believe God has called me to be a single woman. I don't see marriage in my future."

"Why?" Granted, he wasn't going to be her husband, but the woman had a lot to offer a man. It would be a shame for her to live her life single. At least he had a good reason why he would remain single.

"It's like I said, I believe God is leading me that way."

"How do you know?"

"Look at me, Jared. I'm thirty-five years old. My biological clock is ticking. . ." She cut herself off.

There was more, he knew it, but it wasn't really his business to pry, was it? "Alex, you can't go second-guessing God."

"I'm not. I'm accepting, or trying to accept His will for me."

He felt her reasoning was askew, but how could he tell her? "I don't see that, but it's your life. I really don't know you all that well, so I'll leave it alone. As for me, well there are reasons why I can't get involved."

"What are they?"

Jared swallowed hard. "I was engaged once."

"What happened?"

"She died. She died three days before the wedding."

"Oh, Jared, I'm so sorry." Alex's heart lurched. She had known there were things in his past, but she had never guessed that. "Tell me what happened?"

"Hannah had an aneurysm in her brain."

Alex closed her eyes. She knew what that was, she knew the pain, the process. "I'm sorry," she whispered.

"I blamed God for taking Hannah away from me. Then not too many years later, I lost both my parents in a freak accident."

She took his hand; she had to comfort him in some way.

"When I was lost at sea, I made peace with God about my losses, but I could never open myself up to another again. I know I could never survive another loss."

And he thinks my reasons for believing God wanting me single are wrong. "Jared, you won't necessarily lose the next person you love."

"Maybe. I can't take the risk. So you see, no matter how attracted I may be to you or you may be to me, we can never be anything more than friends."

He's attracted to me. Alex squelched a smile. "Tell me, are you better than Job?"

"What?"

"You know, Job, in the Bible."

"I know who you're talking about, I just don't see the connection."

"Well the way I see it, your life, in a way, was like Job's. You had Hannah, your parents, life was going well. Then your world crashes in. You lose Hannah, you lose your parents, you're lost at sea, the sun and the salt eating away at your flesh. All sounds very familiar to me."

Jared simply raised his right eyebrow. He was definitely not liking where she was going with this.

"Don't you see, after the time of testing, God provided Job with a new family. He can do the same for you. If you allow Him."

He didn't speak for several moments, or was it minutes? Time seemed to be dragging by.

"Jared?"

"Sorry, I was thinking. Maybe, but I'm not ready."

"How long ago did Hannah die?" It had to be some time ago, she knew; even the shipwreck was over five years back.

"Fourteen years ago."

"Well maybe it's time."

"Maybe, but I'm not ready."

"Fair enough."

"Alex, I like you, I like you a lot. You fascinate me in more ways than I can put into words but I, we, well, we can't get involved."

"I agree." She smiled. "I wasn't saying you and I should get involved, you know. Only that you shouldn't be closed to the possibility with *anyone*."

He shrugged, absorbing her words. "But, I don't want to lose our friendship. I'm getting used to having someone around. I love your hunger for learning new things."

He loves something about me, at least. What does it matter? You're not going to allow yourself to fall for this man either. Relax, Alex, keep this in perspective. "I want us to be friends too."

"So, how do we do this?"

"We keep our hands to ourselves?" *And definitely our lips.* The kiss came flooding back to her memory; she fought it down.

"Agreed."

"We're adults, Jared. This shouldn't be a problem." Who was she going to kid? Every ounce of her being wanted to get to know the man beside her. It was wrong to want that, she knew. Being single forever, she couldn't help but hope she was adult enough to keep her impulses under control with God's help.

His smile nervously crept up his cheek. *Maybe he's not sure he can handle his emotional responses, like me.* He nodded his head but didn't say a word.

Alex rose to clear the dinner dishes. "The lobster was great, Jared, thanks."

"Welcome. That reminds me, I should call Stan."

"You're welcome to use my phone, if it's working, of course."

Jared walked over to the kitchen phone. "It's activated."

Alex nodded and continued cleaning up the dishes. Jared helped while he held the phone to his ear by his shoulder. She tried not to listen, but his easy conversation with his friend was obvious. There was so much about him that intrigued her.

She filled the sink with hot soapy water and began to wash. Jared stepped up to the sink beside her and dried. He placed each dish, glass, silverware, and pot into its rightful spot. *How often had he been in this house?* she wondered. He was so at home here.

"Brad and Phyllis!" she nearly shouted.

"What?" Jared said as he hung up the phone.

"Brad and Phyllis must be going nuts. I'm sure they heard about the storm."

"I better call them." Jared tapped out the Trainers' number.

"Brad, it's Jared. Fine. Some, a little to the roof, but I'll have that repaired in no time." Jared's hand touched his wound. Alex's stomach tightened, her knees locked. She had forgotten about his injuries. Maybe tonight wasn't such a good night to discuss their kiss.

"Alex is fine. The boat? Nothing that can't be redone. . . Thanks, hopefully by spring."

Jared sat down at the table. "No, I hadn't heard that."

Alex made her way to her room; it was too easy to eavesdrop. After all, she needed a break from Jared. He couldn't seem to move or say anything that didn't awaken senses. *Lord, this is going to be the hardest test You've ever put me through. Please give me the strength and grace to endure.*

"Alex!" Jared hollered. His hand was cupped over the mouthpiece when she came back in the room. "Brad wants to speak with you. I'm going home. I'll see you tomorrow, okay?"

She nodded and then took the phone. "Hi, Brad, how's everyone?"

੩₰

Jared was out the door and catching his breath as the chill of the evening air hit him in the chest. He had to workout. Days had passed since his last workout, and his body craved the exercise. He didn't exercise by going to a gym; he simply did push-ups and pull-ups, one-handed of course.

At his cottage he worked his muscles until they ached. It felt good, the blood pumping through his veins, his muscles bulging in all the right places. Although never having competed, he had been tempted a time or two. But his father's caution about vanity and temptation of worldly pursuits had always kept him away.

His thoughts wandered to the house up the hill, to a certain woman with Caribbean-blue eyes and chestnut hair. *Does she like how I look? Stop it, Jared, this is dangerous territory*, he told himself. He remembered her fingers tentatively exploring his shoulders. "Oh, Lord, Alex said we are adults and can handle this. I'm not so sure. I don't think the temptation to drink ocean water while I was stranded was a greater temptation than to touch that woman's sweet and wonderful lips. Why, Lord? Why did You put her in my path?"

God didn't seem to be answering.

The sheen of sweat over his body spoke of the need for a second shower. Later, dressed in his pajama bottoms, he took out his Bible and read his daily reading. After those passages he moved over to the book of Job and began to read. *Could it be God is testing me as He tested Job? No, I'm not worthy, not nearly as righteous as Job*. He closed his eyes in prayer, his Bible open across his lap. His mind whirled with questions and confusion, with Scripture and prayer.

His stomach knotted as Alex's comparison of him with Job sprang to life again.

"Am I ready to trust God again?"

ten

For the next month Alex and Jared maintained minimal contact with each other. They waved or spoke briefly about the weather and other trivial things. It was November now, early winter was settling in, and the holidays were around the corner. Alex would soon be flying home for a month. She had promised her parents she would return and spend the holidays with them.

In spite of the fact that she and Jared weren't really talking, she didn't want to leave him alone for the holidays. How could she approach this? Maybe she should stay? No, she couldn't; she promised her folks. She wrapped a warm wool sweater around her and headed to the boathouse.

"Hi." She marveled at all the work Jared had accomplished on the boat. The hull was finished. He was inside the boat and working below.

"Hi."

"I was wondering what you were doing for the holidays?"

"Same as always. I go off the island and spend it with my sister and her family."

"Oh, okay." *See, he doesn't need you,* she chastised herself.

"What about yourself?"

"I'm flying back to Kansas."

"I thought you were staying for a year."

"I am, but I promised my folks I'd return for the holidays."

"So you're coming back?"

She nodded. Maybe he was still interested in her friendship.

"Jared, can we go out to dinner somewhere? Not a date, just as friends. I've missed your company."

"I've missed yours too. And, yeah, dinner sounds fine. I know a few nice restaurants."

"I'm sure you do." She laughed and wagged her head. Man, did she miss his humor. "So what's a good time for you?"

"How's six sound?"

"Sounds great." She waved a hand at the boat. "She's looking good, Jared. When do you hope to launch her?" She rubbed her hand across the stern.

"Not until spring. I'm hoping to get the hull painted before the temps get below freezing, then during the winter I'll work on the galley."

"Too bad this wall was missing—you could have a heater in here."

"I may put up a tarp, depends on the winter. Some are mild, some are bitter cold. How's your research going?"

"Well, I've read just about everything in the historical society on the Luces, and the early 1800s. I'm thinking when I return I'll concentrate on the island after Elizabeth Luce O'Connor left."

"So the island itself is interesting you now?"

"Yup, it's a fascinating place. In Kansas our history only goes back to the 1850s. There are a few records of the Indians and early explorers, but not nearly enough to quench my appetite for history. Here it goes back three hundred and fifty years and more."

"Well, when you're on your next search of island history, remind me to tell you about the time the entire island population became pirates."

"Pirates?"

"Yup, I came across it when I was researching various

ships. It's a really funny story."

"You've got my curiosity piqued. How about telling me over dinner?"

"Sounds like a plan. I'll pick you up at six, okay?"

❧

Jared arrived promptly at six. He knocked on the door and waited, timid about his approach to her. *We need to take this slow and easy*, he thought. "Ready?"

"Most of the way. I'm trying to decide if I need my long wool coat or my down jacket."

"It's a little chilly but still a nice night. Where we are going to eat is down-island and away from the shore, much warmer."

"Where are we going?"

"Vineyard Haven, a place called Louis's. Good food." *And no romantic atmosphere*, he said to himself. *The place will be safe.*

Alex settled on her coat and hung the jacket back up. "Ready."

"Great." Jared held the door open for her, then thought twice about it. He saw Alex raise her eyebrows. "My momma raised me to be a gentleman. Sorry."

"I'll have to thank your momma when I get to heaven. Being a gentleman is a lost art today, I'm afraid."

"It's hard, so many women would just as soon take your head off than find out you hold the door for older men and children too."

"I know. I have a couple of friends like that. Funny, deep down, I think many of them like men opening the door for them. They think of themselves as special in a man's eye just by virtue of being a woman."

"Well, my dear, you are the weaker sex and we are to treat

you with respect. What's that old saying? God didn't take woman out of Adam's foot so that she was beneath him, nor out of his head so that she was above him, but out of his rib so that she was equal but close to his heart."

"I like that. So tell me about Louis's."

"It's in what used to be a residential home. The food's great. He's open year-round, which makes him popular, and the prices are reasonable."

Alex nodded her head. She was beautiful, but he stayed in control. It was nice having her riding beside him, talking with him. It had been too long. They both had not made much effort to talk since the day they shared that kiss. The memory of it still seared his lips. But he was in control now, he was certain of it.

"When do I get to hear about the pirate story?"

"Hmm, let's savor it over dinner."

"Oh, Jared, you can be such a tease when you want to. I'm dying to hear about this, and you know it."

"Maybe." Yes he did know it, and he was teasing her, but he felt the story would be great dinner conversation and would keep them on calm waters.

"How long has your family been on the Vineyard?" Her voice was steady but not angry.

"You know, I've never done a genealogy on my family. I know my mom was a Norton, and there are Nortons quite a ways back. I'm not sure about the Madeiras line, though."

"I've long since moved in my research from direct descendants to some aunts, uncles, and cousins. It's really fascinating. By the way, Nancy Luce, the one with the chickens, was a distant cousin."

"I'm sure that's a relief. You wouldn't want craziness running through your blood now, would you?" He winked.

"You know, she wasn't crazy, just eccentric."

"Eccentric, my dear, was the term once used to describe family members with Alzheimer's and other forms of dementia."

"True, but she seemed to have the rest of her faculties in place. Just those silly chickens were unusual."

"She must have been lonely. Who else have you found out about?"

"Well, there was a Jonathan Luce who loved to dress in very rich clothing. When he traveled to Boston they referred to him as Count Luce because of his finery."

"So vanity runs in your family lines."

"He probably got it from Captain Thomas's wife. She spoke of her husband as 'merely the son of a woodcutter' and always spoke of him as 'the Captain.' "

"You know, the women referred to their spouses in a very formal way when they were in public, and even in their own homes in front of the children. Familiarity with one's spouse, calling him by his first name for example, was for the bedroom only." *Bedroom, oops! What was I thinking? I shouldn't have referred to that.* Jared concentrated on the road ahead of him. The moon was out, the sky was clear; hardly anyone was out tonight.

"I know, so strange, so different from our culture today. My parents showed their affection to each other in front of the kids, lots of kisses and hugs."

"Same with mine. Speaking of folks, when will you be seeing yours?" There, back to a safe subject.

"I leave a couple days before Thanksgiving."

"Need a ride to the airport? I'll be glad to take you—that way you won't have to leave your car parked there for a month."

"I may take you up on that, thanks."

Jared pulled the car into a parking space behind the restaurant. "Here we are."

Jared led the way, careful not to wrap his arm around her as he was inclined to do. So many little things he needed to guard himself against. He could make this work, he assured himself, and opened the door to the restaurant for her.

ຈ

Alex was amazed; the amount of tables and chairs in the place was mind boggling. The restaurant was about half full. Smells wafting past her nostrils made her stomach gurgle and her mouth water. Jared was right, the food would be good. She noted, with relief, that it was not a romantic place. There were too many tables in one common room. She was thankful that he was trying just as hard as she was to remain friends. Nothing more, nothing less. She did so enjoy his friendship. He was such a knowledgeable man. Not at all the sort of person she had thought he was when they met the first day. How could she have ever called him a Neanderthal? She followed Jared behind a pleasant hostess to a table.

"It smells great."

"I think you'll enjoy the food."

Alex opened the menu and scanned it. She settled on the fettucini, Jared on a large steak. Once their orders were placed, she met his eyes. Did she dare ask him again about the pirates?

"Okay, okay, I see it in your eyes, you want to know about the pirates."

"Well, how about it?" *How can he read my eyes so well?* Alex stifled the growing realization of the connection between them. It was obvious, no matter how cool they played the game.

"Well, back in 1918, during World War One, there was a British ship bound for New York. It was to meet up with a caravan of other ships bringing supplies to the troops in France. This ship, the *Port Hunter*, left from Boston. As she sailed passed the Vineyard, a tugboat rammed her. I'm assuming it was foul weather, but I don't rightly know how and why a tugboat could ram the vessel. I just know it wasn't intentional."

Their drinks came. Alex took a sip of her cola. "And?"

"Well, the captain knew of the shoals off the Vineyard and ran the ship over them. This would allow for the recovery of the cargo, if not the recovery of the vessel itself."

"Sounds smart."

"It should have been. I got the account from old Stan Lair who was a teen at the time. He had gone into town one day and saw all these British sailors. So he's looking in the harbor for their boat, but there wasn't any. He starts asking around and finds out about the ship sinking. According to Stan, it didn't take long for things to start floating up on shore."

"What kinds of things?"

"Crates full of clothing for the army, candles, mess kits, anything and everything a soldier would need."

"So what's this got to do with pirating?"

"Well, in Stan's words, somehow one of the cargo holds must have popped open and the cargo started to float. That 'somehow' must have been one of the locals. Where the boat lay on the shoals, the water was nearly waist deep if you were walking on the deck. Wouldn't take much for someone to walk in the water and pop the hold."

"No, I imagine it wouldn't. But still, pirates?"

"Hang on, dear, there's plenty of piracy that went on. Only

thing is, no one quite saw it like that. Seems the locals were taking their boats and fishing in the hold, pulling out crates, anything that would float. In some of these crates were leather vests. They'd sell them in the harbor for a buck apiece, the black leather jackets went for two dollars."

"Isn't that salvaging rights?"

"Not exactly. The company, or the government, finally sent some men to investigate. But by the time they did, all the clothing and floatable crates were long off the vessel. There were boats coming in from New Bedford to purchase the ill-gotten goods."

The waiter came with their plates and placed their meals in front of them. Alex took a mouthful of the fettucini, and groaned in pleasure.

"Good, huh?"

"Wonderful. Please continue."

"Well, old Stan said he and a couple of boys later that day had heard some of the crates were floating up on shore, so they went down to check it out. There was this one old guy pulling in crates, writing his initials on them, but then a group of others hiding in the bushes took the crates from him."

"Good grief!"

"Exactly. It gets worse. Not only were they pulling things in off the shore, they were pulling them off of the boat as well. Fishing took on a whole new venue. You've heard of the illustrious 'box fish,' haven't you?"

"They tried to call it that?"

"No, that's my take on the whole thing. Back then there were about four thousand island residents. Stan said that nearly everyone got in on the act, whether it was the hauling of loot off the boat or the selling of it. He said eventually the leather coats got up to five bucks apiece."

"You're kidding."

"Nope, that's a fact. The price was so high, if you had purchased a jacket and had it drying on your line, you'd lose it. He even said that not only would your jacket be stolen, but the rest of your laundry too."

"What people will do for money. What happened when the officials came?"

"Best as I can piece it all together, the islanders all became ignorant. No one was going to tell on their neighbor or family member."

"So no one got caught?"

"Not that I saw in the records."

"That's amazing."

"They managed to recover a few small things, but nothing of significance. Stan also said that several houses were built off the profits from that boat. He called the whole island a bunch of pirates. I think he included himself right along with 'em, too."

Alex laughed. The thought of stealing someone's laundry was a hoot. "So is this Stan a relative of yours?"

"Mine? My dear are you asking if I'm a descendant of a pirate?"

Alex pictured Jared, dressed in old sea captain clothes, the Hollywood representation of one, of course. She could imagine the bright bold colors, his shirt open, exposing his bronze chest, a sash for a belt, and him standing on the deck calling out orders. He was the captain of course in her fantasy; she smirked at her overactive imagination.

"What? What on earth is going on in that pretty little head of yours?"

"Oh nothing, just picturing pirates with swords and a captain giving orders."

"Ah-hah."

She didn't say more. She figured he'd read her mind if she let on anything else. "So were there any Luces involved with this pirating adventure?"

"I'm certain, but I couldn't tell you who."

"I'll have to look that up. Thankfully, my line left the island before this, so I'm not the descendant of any pirate."

"I see. So I'm the rogue of society because my ancestors went crazy over some ill-gotten gain?"

"Could be. Tell me, is that why salt flows through your veins?"

"That, and probably the fact that I've grown up on the water. I can't get enough of it. I was on the mainland for a few years while I attended college. It was too far inland. The only water I found was fresh. It was pretty, don't get me wrong, but it lacked a little character not having salt in it."

"I see, so salt is the essence of life."

"My dear doctor, you more than anyone must know."

"Know what?"

"How many parts saline solution we are."

He'd done it again, amazed her with his knowledge. He was right, the human body was primarily made up of saline solution. "Touché, Jared, touché."

eleven

The holidays went by quickly. When the time came to leave, she hated to leave her parents, but she was anxious to get back to the Vineyard to see Jared again. She had to admit it to herself, she was in love with the man. There was no denying it—but there was no point in proclaiming it either. He was not interested in a relationship and never would be. She had to admit to her mom, who read her like a book, that she had a fondness for Jared. Even though she never said the word "love," she was certain her mother knew.

If she hadn't talked about him so often maybe her parents wouldn't have suspected anything. She explained to her mother the situation with Jared and his desires never to love again, to which her mother simply stated, "If God has destined for you two to fall in love, there will be no stopping it, no matter how hard either of you try. Stop being so foolish. At thirty-five one doesn't play games." Unfortunately, she'd had to agree with her mother, but when she thought of Jared and the possibility of him opening his heart to her, it all seemed pointless.

Maybe she should stay in Kansas. Her practice was going well. She spent some time with her patients and realized they loved Dr. Bob, and he loved them also. She missed her work, but not as much as she missed Jared.

Alex's stomach tightened as she gripped the shoulder strap of her carry-on bag and hustled through the airport. When had she fallen so hard for Jared that he was more important to her than her patients? *Oh, Lord, help me out here. I don't know what to do!*

She boarded the plane back to the Vineyard. The farms, covered with snow, with their little specks of houses and cattle, passed silently beneath her. What was she going to say to Jared when she returned? *I missed you and oh, by the way, I'm in love with you.* No, she couldn't do that. Alex chewed on a nail until the polish was off. She hadn't chewed her nails since high school. *Maybe in New York I should just turn around and go back.*

"No, it's time to grow up, face my fears, face his too."

"What dear?" a frumpy little old lady sitting beside her asked.

"Sorry. I was thinking to myself. I didn't realize I had spoken out loud."

The woman nodded her head and didn't pry, but she tapped Alex's hand with her own well-wrinkled, soft skin. "God will get you through, dear. He always has for me. Sometimes, I wasn't so pleased with the length of time He took, but in the end He seemed to know what He was doing."

Alex smiled. "I suppose He does, doesn't He?"

"Yes."

"Where are you heading?" she inquired of the elderly woman. Probably going to visit her grandchildren, Alex assumed.

"Me, well I'm meeting up with an old friend. He and I used to date back in high school. His wife passed away several years back and, well, my Vincent, he died nearly ten years ago."

Alex saw the twinkle in the woman's eye. "Are you going to refire a lost love?"

"Oh goodness, I don't know, dear. We dated, just casually.

He had dreams and I had another set of dreams. My Vincent was my soulmate. We had five beautiful children together, and we now have sixteen grandchildren and a couple great-grandchildren. Jason is an old friend. I don't see us being romantically involved. . .but you never know. Right?" She gave Alex a knowing look.

Alex blushed.

"Come on now, dear, I may not be the pretty little thing I was when I was a teen, but when you're older, friendship is of primary importance. Sex, well it's great in a marriage, one of God's gifts. But the best part in a marriage is friendship. To have your spouse be your best friend, that's the key to a happy marriage."

"I suppose you're right. I've never married."

"Why not, dear? You're pretty. I'm sure there were men who were interested in you."

"Oh, there were, I just didn't notice them the way a woman wants to notice her husband. At least, no one until now."

"So you've found him?"

"Yes, but he doesn't want to get involved with anyone, ever."

The elderly woman took Alex's hand into hers. "Dear, few men want to get involved, it just happens. You can't make it and he can't stop it. Love is a very strong gift from God. If this is the man, God will work it out."

"Thanks, I suppose He will. I'd given up on finding some-one, figured I was to be single all my life."

"Tell me, have you read the Bible?"

"All the time." Alex grinned.

"So you're aware of what the apostle Paul says about being single as a gift from God. Tell me, has the Lord specif-ically called you to be single? I'm not talking feelings, I'm talking about an absolute, beyond the shadow of a doubt calling from God."

Who was this woman? How could she ask such direct questions? The heat on Alex's face started to sting. "No, I just assumed it because of my age."

"Then it's simply a case of waiting on the Lord. I realize, dear, you are feeling your age, but our age means nothing to the Lord."

"I suppose."

"Trust me, dear. Why do you suppose God had me sit beside you today?"

Why *had* that happened? She could have sat next to anyone and yet here was a woman who was older and wiser, who understood her fears. Having lived longer, this woman was forward and yet truthful. Obviously this encounter was God-ordained. "Because I needed reassurance?"

"I call it encouragement. I suppose it's the gift of exhortation, but it's not like I was correcting you for going down the wrong path. Although self-doubt is a problem. Trust the Lord with all your heart, dear. You know the verse."

"And lean not on your own understanding."

"Yes, and He will make your paths straight. I've taken many detours in my life, I'm afraid. But God has always been faithful to pull me back, showing me the right path."

"Thanks."

"Thank the Lord, dear. So, tell me about this handsome hunk of a man that's driving you crazy."

Alex laughed.

≈

Jared paced the small building known as the Martha's Vineyard Airport terminal. Her plane was supposed to be on time. It had left New York on time. The knot in the middle of his gut intensified. "Lord, please keep her safe." Twenty minutes had crawled by since her plane was scheduled to land. Tempted to inquire again, but embarrassed about being a pest, he resisted pursuing the matter. He had asked twice already. Two planes had landed since he had arrived, enough to get his hopes raised and dashed.

Jared had been miserable during Alex's absence. Never had he missed someone so much. It was funny how accustomed he was to just having her around. Her laughter, her smile, the cute little dimple on her left cheek. . . Everything about her was so vivid in his mind. He knew he was caring too much for this woman, he knew he was sinking, and yet he still wanted to hold on. It wasn't like he wanted to get married or anything. No, he just wanted a friendship. Someone who was his confidante.

A commuter plane's wheels screeched as it landed on the tarmac in front of him. As it taxied around, he walked over to the counter. The woman behind it nodded. Hustling out the doors, he reached the gate. The plane's door slowly opened. He strained to see if Alex was on board. His heart pounded. At last, nothing stood between him and his desire to see her once again.

A smile broadened across his face. There she was, just as he had remembered her. Her long chocolate-brown hair, tropical-blue eyes, and the way her smile lit up her face. He waved. She returned the gesture.

He hopped the wooden split-rail fence that made up the gate and traversed the distance between them. "Hi, let me get those bags for you."

"Thanks."

"How was your flight?" Jared slung her suitcase strap over his shoulder.

"Fine, except there was a bit of turbulence between here and New York."

"You must be exhausted—that's a long day of travel."

"I'll sleep well tonight. How are you?"

"Fine. Boy you're a sight for sore eyes." He searched her delicate face. *Had she missed him too?* he wondered.

She rubbed the back of her neck. "Thanks, it's good to see you too."

"How many bags are we waiting for?"

"Just a couple. Did you bring my car or your truck?"

"I took yours."

"Great. I'm going to need to do some shopping before we go back."

"It's all taken care of."

"Jared?"

"It's my welcome home gift for you. Relax, enjoy. Besides, I figured I can get a meal or two out of you for it."

"You did, did you?" Her smiled deepened. "Well, if you bought enough, I'm sure you can. You do have quite an appetite."

"But there isn't an ounce of fat on me, Doc. You have to admit, I don't overeat."

"Maybe. Maybe you simply exercise harder when you've pigged out."

"I'll never tell," he teased. Man, he'd missed her and the playful bantering between them. He ambled up to the luggage cart that had just been unloaded from the plane. Her bags were full, but the volume of weight was not a problem. The size of the bags, and balancing them in his arms—that took a little more finesse. "Did you bring home some of Kansas?"

"Just a little. I've a little something for you in one of the bags."

"A present, you brought me a present?"

"Yes, you mean to tell me you didn't buy me one?"

Jared laughed. "You know, I did, but it's at the house. You'll have to wait."

"In that case you'll have to wait too."

Jared loaded the bags in the back end of the Bronco. "Would you like to drive or would you like me to?"

"You can drive, I'm beat."

Inside the car, her delicate perfume tantalized his senses. He still hadn't put a name to the scent. He had been tempted to check out her perfumes while she was away, but he'd thought better of it. His thoughts shifted to the gift he'd purchased. He hoped she would like her present. It was a bold one, but he hoped she wouldn't mind. He figured at the very worst he could keep it if she wasn't pleased.

"So, how's the boat coming?"

"I can't do too much on her now. The weather has been uncooperative."

"Did you put up that temporary wall?"

"Yes, but it's still been too windy. There's been a lot of arctic air from the north." Jared turned right and headed for home. "So tell me, how are your folks, the farm?"

"My parents are great. They want to come to the Vineyard. I don't know if they'll get a chance this summer or not, but they'll be planning a visit."

"Great, you can show them the sights."

"Naturally. I know just about everything on this island now."

"Oh, really? Tell me, doctor, where are the nude beaches?"

"What?"

"Not that you or I would be going, but it's good to know where they are so you don't accidentally come across them."

"They allow that sort of thing here?"

"It's a privately owned beach, but somehow along the way it became a nude beach. Unfortunately, many tourists seek it out."

"Well please tell me where and how to avoid it."

"I'll show you."

"Jared, I don't want to go there."

"No, we pass it on the way home."

"We do? I drive this road all the time, I never, I mean how. . . ?"

"Hang on, there isn't a sign saying 'this way to the nude beach.' Word gets around and people flock."

"That's sad."

"Yup."

When they passed the road to the beach Jared pointed it out.

"That's so huge."

"Isn't it? When I was just a kid it was a footpath. About twenty years ago it got so popular they widened the road. Too many people were getting stuck trying to get around each other. Eventually it became what you see now, with two lanes and room on each side to park. The owners now charge people for access."

"Wow, it's hard to believe sin can make so much money, but it does, time and time again. You read about it, see it, even the Bible talks about it."

"Sin is profitable, but death is certain because of it." Jared looked over at her. "Alex, don't you see sin in your practice of medicine?"

"Yes, I hate it. But it's a part of caring for others. You see the evidence of sin everywhere. Children beaten to death, or near death, burned, whipped, raped. . .it's very, very sad. I'm thankful that most of my patients' families are not like that. It's hard to witness that kind of abuse of children."

"It's very hard, I know. Unfortunately, I dealt with it with Hannah and her family. She had an uncle that needed help. The family got it for him and, as far as I know he's doing fine now."

"We live in tough times."

Jared turned on to the Trainers' driveway. "On another note, your present, well, it may attack you."

"What?" *What on earth did he get me?* she wondered.

"Attack is probably too strong a word. Let's just say it might be excited to see you. Of course, it could be terrified to see you also."

"Jared, what did you do?"

"I took a chance. It's a demanding gift. Something that will take lots of your time and gives little in return, and yet it gives so much."

Other than an animal of some sort she wasn't sure what he was talking about. *But he wouldn't buy me an animal, would he? He knows I work long hours. My work, my life isn't good for an animal. He couldn't have, could he?* "Don't tell me you bought me an animal?"

"Not quite."

"How do you 'not quite' buy an animal? You either did or you didn't."

They sat in the parked car, her eyes searching his. He was up to something. Something mischievous, if she could tell correctly. "Jared. . ."

"Come on, I'll show you."

He opened the door to her house to find a bouncing pup of gold leap out. *A dog, the man bought me a dog. How could he? But he's so cute.* Alex knelt down on the porch. "Does he have a name?"

"Captain."

"Captain?"

"Yup, you came here in search of a captain—it seemed only fitting."

He was so right. She came in search of Captain Thomas Luce on her first trip, and now she came in search of another captain—Jared. She ducked her head so he wouldn't read her thoughts. "Come here, Captain."

The puppy pounced over to her and licked her face, his tail wagging back and forth. His fur was soft like silk. "What kind of dog is it?"

"It's a he, and he's a golden retriever, about three months old."

"He's adorable. But, Jared, I don't have a life that's fair to an animal."

"You do here. If you can't take him back to Kansas, I understand, and I'll raise him. While you're here, you can enjoy him, can't you?"

With every part of her being she wanted to enjoy this puppy. She loved animals, she loved dogs. Did he know that retrievers were said to be the best dogs for children? "It doesn't seem fair to the dog, to have him get attached to me and then leave him." *But maybe she wouldn't have to leave him. Maybe she and Jared would get together and then there would be two people to care for the dog. . .*

"It's not like Captain won't know me. I'll be around. He'll adjust if you have to leave him."

Adjust, just like Jared had adjusted to living single the rest of his life. "Thanks, Jared, I love dogs, I really do but. . ."

"Please, don't say no just yet. Let him grow on you. He'll be great for companionship. He'll love to walk the beach with you."

So Jared was aware that she walked the beach nearly every

morning. "Okay, how can I turn down those wonderful round puppy eyes?"

"They're great eyes, aren't they? Such a deep brown. Reminds me of your hair."

"Actually I was referring to your puppy eyes, but Captain has great puppy eyes too." That should set him off balance just a touch. Alex smiled as Jared's eyes widened. She'd scored another point, hitting him in a way he hadn't expected. *Why do I like doing that to him so much, keeping him off balance?*

She rose from her knees and proceeded into the house. "Come on boy, and bring your friend."

"Are you talking to the dog or me?"

"The Captain," she winked.

≈

The dog might have been a mistake; never had he seen Alex so bold in her affection. *And just who was she talking to just then, me or the dog?* Muttering, he said under his breath, "Captain, I think we're heading into stormy waters. Brace yourself, boy!"

twelve

Captain was growing in leaps and bounds, and Jared, true to his word, spent as much time with the animal as possible. They seemed as close as Alex and Captain were.

Every morning Captain would join her for her walks down the beach. Occasionally he would catch a sand crab. He loved to bark and paw at the poor things. Of course, they held their own against their loud attacker, and more than once Alex had to clean wounds on Captain's nose.

He was a great companion. She could confide in him when her heart ached to tell Jared the truth of her love for him. But that wasn't to be. He was still as confident in his resolve not to get involved as he had been before she left for Kansas.

Spring was in the air, and the crocuses popped their white and purple heads out of the ground. The days were brighter and definitely warmer, the wind ceased blowing from the north as often, coming more from the west or occasionally from the south. The buds on the oak trees were peeking out.

Captain would spend his days with Jared when Alex went down-island to work on her research. But she was going less and less. Instead, she spent more of her time at the house, working with Jared on the boat. She was so proud of him and his talent with his hands. The boat was beautiful. It still had some work before it was finished, but it was nearly ready to be launched.

The colder days, Jared spent with her and Captain, showing her some island sights and helping her with research.

"Mrs. Arno, how long have you been working here at the historical society?" Alex inquired one day. It wasn't like she could ask her curious questions about Jared straight-out; that would simply imply too much.

"Goodness, Alex, it's been fifteen years since I retired from teaching. Call me Beatrice, dear."

"Okay, tell me. . ." Alex searched for the right words. "Do you know a Jared Madeiras?"

"Ah, yes. I had Jared in my class; he was a bright boy. . . loved reading and history but like most kids he had a hard time doing all his homework."

"Oh really?"

"Funny how that happens. I mean, when he was a youngster he did only what he had to do. Now, however, the man is very thorough in his research. Much like you are dear. So, tell me, where'd you meet Jared?"

Alex felt her face flame. "He's the caretaker of the place where I'm living."

"Oh, so you're staying in the Trainers' home."

"Yes."

"He's a good man, Alex. He's had some tragedy in his life but he's honest, trustworthy, and a hard worker. Not to mention he's a pretty handsome specimen of the male species too." Beatrice winked and headed back to her research.

Well that was obvious, Alex, she chastised herself, then attempted to concentrate on the papers before her. Today Alex had spring fever worse than she had ever known it before, even worse than in college. She didn't want to work, she didn't want to read, she simply wanted to take the day off and relax, enjoy the sunshine, and be totally free of commitments. She hurried home to Captain's greeting.

"Come here, boy, want to go visit Jared?" The dog wagged

his tail so hard his backend wiggled with it. She loved this dog so much.

"Let's go get 'im." Alex opened the screen door and the dog was off, running down the porch and heading toward the boathouse. He was in a full run as she rounded the corner. She heard a whistle and turned.

It was Jared. She looked back at Captain, who tumbled trying to stop himself. Back on his feet and clawing his way back, he sniffed the air. His head turned in the direction where Jared stood, and he barked.

"Come on, boy," Jared called out.

Captain was in a full run again in a matter of seconds. Alex laughed. The poor dog had so much energy. He was getting bigger, but he still had some growing left in him. He would to be a good-size dog.

Captain pranced up and down around Jared. "Where's Mommy, boy?"

Captain stood alert and his snout pointed in Alex's direction. "Get her, Captain," Jared pointed toward Alex.

The dog came barreling back to her. She patted him, "Good boy, you found him." She was so tempted to call Jared "Daddy," but that would make her fantasy of them getting together too real, too hard to deal with on a day-to-day basis.

"Hey, Alex, how are you this morning?"

"Lousy."

Jared put down his wood cutter, his voice alarmed. "What's the matter?"

"Nothing, really, just a bad case of spring fever."

"Ahh, I know the cure."

"What?"

"Pack an overnight bag and a picnic lunch."

"You're crazy."

"Probably. Come on, Alex, it will be fun. Don't you trust me?"

"I trust you. Do I need warm clothes, coats, gloves—anything else?"

"All that, plus pack some food for Captain."

"Okay."

"I'll be back in an hour or so. Be ready."

"Where are we going, Jared?"

"It's a surprise, trust me."

"Okay. Do you want to take Captain with you?"

"Sure. Come on, Captain, we've got work to do."

The dog left her side and followed Jared. Alex scratched her head. What on earth could he possibly have in mind that involved an overnight bag?

છે

Jared drove his old truck toward Menemsha, eventually pulling into John Poole's scallop-shelled drive. The shells were so old and weathered they had become small chunks of sun-bleached shells now. "Hey, Jared, what brings you out this morning?"

"Need a favor, John."

"Anything. What's up?"

"I want to take Alex to New Bedford. Can I borrow your boat?"

"Sure, let me get the keys. Both tanks are full. I think the water is probably too shallow at your dock, though."

"I agree. I'll leave the truck in the parking lot."

"When ya coming back?"

"Probably tomorrow night. It's still too cold to take her over in my boat, but your cabin cruiser with the wheelhouse enclosed will be like a luxury liner."

"You know, Dr. Tucker has been doing all that research on whaling, I bet she'd love the museums over in New Bedford. That was my thinking. Nantucket is another possibility, but it might be better when the weather's warmer."

Captain jumped out of the truck and sidled up beside Jared.

"Hey there, Captain." John reached out to the dog. The golden retriever licked his hand. "Friendly pup, aren't you?" He looked at his friend. "Jared, what are you going to do with the dog?"

"Take him."

John looked down at the dog, pulled his ball cap off, and patted the pup's head. "I don't know, son, seems to me the dog wouldn't be allowed in the museums and stuff."

"I hadn't thought about that."

"Say, I'll watch him for you. I'm sure the wife won't mind."

"You sure? I wouldn't want to put you out."

"I'm sure. Come on, Captain, let's meet the missus." John opened the door for the retriever and he stepped right in. "Martha, we've got company."

"Jared, it's so good to see you." Martha hugged him with a friendly embrace.

"Good to see you too, Martha. Although I'm not the guest John's referring too."

"Oh!" Martha looked at her husband and then at the dog. "John, no, you promised no more animals."

John's belly rolled up and down with laughter. "He's only visiting, honey. He's Jared's."

"Actually, he's Alex's, but we kind of share him."

Martha raised an eyebrow but held her words. Jared thought about correcting her obvious misconception, but he decided that would just take too much time.

"Jared's borrowing the boat to go to New Bedford. I offered to watch Captain for a couple of days, if it's all right with you, of course."

Jared caught John's wink to his wife. A coral blush painted Martha's cheeks and Jared thought how wonderful it was when people stayed in love with each other over the years.

"Oh, John, really, like I could ever say no to you. Come here, Captain." The puppy stomped over to her and wagged his tail. "I take it he's house-trained?"

"Yes, ma'am."

"Then he can stay." She turned to the dog and bent down. "Would you like to visit for a few days, Captain?" she cooed.

Jared went down to one knee. "Captain, you be a good boy, do as John and Martha tell you, okay?"

Captain licked Jared's face and nuzzled into his chest. "I love you, too, boy. I'll see you in a couple of days."

"Thanks, John." He extended his hand. "Thanks for everything."

"No problem. Here's the keys. Have fun."

"I think we will."

Jared kissed Martha on her cheek and returned to his truck. *Dog food! They're going to need dog food. We can drop it off on our way to the boat.* He rushed back home, packed an overnight bag, plopped it into the rear of his truck, and drove up the hill to Alex's. He hadn't even reached the door when she opened it to him.

৯

She looked around. "Where's Captain?"

"At some friends'. Where we're going we might have trouble taking a dog."

"Jared, where *are* we going, and *who* has my dog?"

"John and Martha Poole. You met John once when he was helping me on the boat."

John seemed like a nice enough man, and if Jared trusted him with Captain, he must be. But still, didn't she have a right to say what did or did not happen with her dog? She squelched the desire to argue with Jared about this. Another time, another place would be better. "I'm ready, I think!" she said, hoping her nervousness didn't show in her smile.

"Relax, trust me."

"I'm trying, Jared, I really am. I'm just not very good with surprises."

"We've got to take Captain some food, so you'll get to say good-bye to him and meet the Pooles in their home."

Somehow this made her feel better. Seeing that Captain was in good hands would help her relax. She grabbed her bag, and Jared carried the dog's food. "Come on, Alex, this is my world-famous cure for spring fever. You're going to have a ball."

"If nothing else, I won't die of boredom."

Jared roared with laughter. It warmed her down to her toes. The idea of spending the day and the next with him was comforting and exciting, both at the same time.

After a brief stop at the Pooles' all of Alex's fears for Captain were laid aside. They were like the perfect grandparents—retired, kind-hearted, and spoiling their grandchildren. Already Martha had given Captain some steak. "Can you believe she was feeding him steak?"

"Yup, they're good folks, Alex. They've been like a set of grandparents to me."

"Are your grandparents still alive?"

"No. Well, I'm not sure. My grandmother died a while back, before my folks did. My grandfather, well, he was another story. Seems like family responsibilities got to be too much and he just up and sailed off one day. I really don't know much about it. Dad never liked to talk about it. I guess it was hard on my father. He became the head of the household, quit school, went to work, and provided for the family. My mom's folks I never really knew. I saw them when I was a child a few times, but they died young."

"Goodness, Jared, I don't think I've known anyone with as much death in his family at such a young age."

"I've accepted it. Now, you ready for your surprise?"

Alex looked around. They were at Menemsha harbor, parked toward the beach but facing the wharf. "Yes. What are we doing here?"

"John owns that boat over there."

Alex followed where Jared was pointing to a cabin cruiser with a wheelhouse on top, all blocked in, shining bright in the sunlight. "What are you saying?"

"We're going out to sea, Alex."

"What? It's March, and it's freezing out there on the water!"

"Not really. The boat is heated. It's very modern and quite comfortable. As you can see, the wheelhouse is enclosed so it's warm up there as well."

"Where are we going?"

"Well, that's the second part of the surprise."

"Jared, I don't swim well."

"Relax, we aren't going to sink. Besides, with hypothermia you wouldn't need to swim long anyway."

"Oh, you're horrible." *Great, if we sink, we die from the elements. This is a fun trip*, she thought sarcastically.

"Alex, trust me?"

If she heard him say "trust me" one more time. . .

"Come on, you country farmgirl, you."

I should never have agreed to something I didn't know

about first. I'll never, ever do that again. She grabbed her overnight bag and prayed, *Oh God, please let Jared be as good of a captain as he thinks he is.*

"Nervous?"

"No." Okay, she lied. But no way was she going to tell him otherwise.

"Right. Come on, let me show you around."

Jared helped her aboard. The swaying sensation of the boat beneath her feet felt odd, but the boat settled back in place quickly enough. Jared unlocked the cabin first, and she stepped inside. "Oh my, this is incredible." Before her lay plush carpet, a couch that wrapped around a table with some chairs, a kitchen, and another doorway down a couple of stairs.

"It's nice, isn't it?"

"This is a floating house?"

"Basically, yes. A while back John and Martha retired and lived on board for several years, going to Florida in the winter and back here in the summer. Now they pretty much stay here year-round, but they still go out for long trips every now and again." He pointed. "The bedroom is past those doors, and I'll be staying there tonight. You, on the other hand, will be safe and sound on land."

"What?" she questioned. He started to open his mouth, but she interrupted before he could speak. "Don't you dare say 'trust me' again or so help me, I'll. . ."

He raised his hands in defense. "I promise, I won't say it again. But I've got a plan, okay?"

She wagged her head. "Okay."

Alex watched Jared get ready to leave the dock, removing protective covers, starting the engine, checking everything thoroughly. With each action, her confidence in him and his abilities to captain this boat increased. Finally, he removed the lines and stepped on board. He climbed back up to the wheelhouse and shifted the engine into gear.

The water gurgled off the stern as they pulled away from the dock. Alex joined Jared in the wheelhouse. "This is an amazing view."

"Menemsha's always been one of the prettiest harbors. She's small, but with the pond to our left, the inlet over there toward Lobsterville. . .I don't know, it's just been a special place for me."

"Did you learn to pilot boats in this harbor?"

"Yup. When I was a kid I used to walk down here all the time. I'd spend hours fishing off the docks, catching squid, mackerel, and some junk fish. Once in a while I'd catch a flounder. As a kid, eating the very fish you caught always seemed to taste better."

Alex smiled. His life, his growing up, was so different than hers. "So where are we heading?"

"Have you ever read nautical maps?"

"No."

"Come here, let me show you." Jared pulled out a map that concentrated on the water, its various depths and other markings. It was so unlike a road map, where the land was a simple color with no markings except for place-names. He showed her the path they were taking, how to navigate by the compass.

Once they were out in open waters, Jared put the boat on autopilot, then turned to her and said, "So what did you bring for lunch?"

Alex stared at the man. "Don't you need to watch where we're going?"

"I did. The horizon is clear, autopilot is on, I have a few

minutes before I'll need to check again."

"I'm sorry I'm so nervous. I don't know why—you obviously know what you're doing."

"Come here."

Alex took a step toward him.

He grabbed her shoulders and turned her around. He worked his hands at the nape of her neck and gave her a gentle massage. "I know you read about my accident at sea, but that really was the only time I've had anything major happen."

"Jared, it's not that."

"I know, you weren't brought up on this stuff like I was. To me this is the same as stitching up a laceration would be for you."

She turned back and faced him. They hadn't been this close since the time they had kissed. Everything within her wanted to kiss him again. She searched his eyes. They seemed to be saying the same thing, but she held back.

"Jared, where are we headed?"

thirteen

Was she asking about them as a couple—or about their destination? In either case, he wasn't ready to answer. "After lunch, Alex. I'll tell you then."

"You and your incredible appetite." She winked at him.

"Feed me or I die, it's that simple."

"I doubt that, but I'll get our lunch. Would you like some coffee?"

"That would be great. Thanks."

Jared watched Alex take the stairs. Her hands didn't clutch the rails quite so tightly this time. "You know, I could prepare lunch if you want to stay up here and watch," he called after her.

"I think I'm more comfortable in the kitchen."

"Okay, I'll let you get away with it for now, but later you're steering this vessel." He patted the wheel.

She paled. "I don't think so." The look of terror in her eyes made him more determined to help her break this fear.

Jared scanned the horizon again. Nothing was out there, though way off in the distance he could see some fishing trollers. But they wouldn't be moving across his path. He sat back and prayed, "Father, please help Alex relax and enjoy this gorgeous day."

She returned shortly with a cup of hot coffee. "Jared, they have everything in there. I just boiled the water. I wasn't sure if I could use the microwave or not."

"You can, but it's not as efficient. Usually that's used in

port when you're hooked up to power at a slip."

"Gotcha. I'll be right back."

"Thanks."

When she returned with their food, he stepped away from the wheel and helped her. "Don't you need to hold the wheel?"

"Nope. It's on autopilot," he reminded her. "Watch." Jared saw Alex's eyes widen as the wheel moved back and forth. "Works the same on planes."

"I don't even want to think about that," she mumbled as she stepped onto the upper level of the wheelhouse.

He chuckled; he couldn't help it. "You're a wonder, Doc. You work on the insides of a human being and yet you fear the ocean."

"I know it doesn't make sense but, believe it or not, I'm liking it out here."

"Come on, sit down here." Jared lead her to the captain's chair. He stood behind her and worked her tense muscles around her neck and shoulders.

"You have marvelous hands, Jared."

Her voice, soft and alluring as her scent on the ocean breeze, caressed his heart. He'd come to know her so well. *Maybe we should take this relationship further?* he thought. "Alex. . ."

She turned to him. He knew his gaze was intense. The reaction in her eyes was equal to what he felt in his heart. He explored every freckle, every eyelash, the soft creamy texture of her skin. "Oh, Alex, may I kiss you?"

Tentatively, she reached out to him. She hadn't spoken a word, she didn't need to. He leaned down and drank in her lips, so moist, so tender and sweet, just as he remembered them.

She moaned—or was it him—he wasn't sure. He drew her

closer. There was no denying his attraction to her any longer. They both knew it. They'd been foolish trying to hide it. She placed her hands on his chest. At first they explored him, but now she was pushing him back. He didn't want to stop kissing her, but she was right. He stepped back and released her. Cool air chilled his heated skin. Sitting down in the other deck chair, he waited for her to speak.

৯

Alex closed her eyes and tried to focus. Mind, body, soul, and spirit longed to be back in Jared's embrace. But the fire between them was far too intense. Her self-control was being taxed. He was waiting for her response, but what could. . . should she say? The reaction to their first kiss had been a disaster she didn't want to repeat. "Jared, I like you very much." *Actually I love you, but you're not ready to hear that.* "And I believe you like me. Are you ready to bring our relationship to the next level?"

"Alexandria, you don't know how ready I am. I've wanted to start dating you, get closer to you, but you said you weren't interested."

"Jared, you said the same to me. I've kept you at bay because I thought that's what you wanted." *You mean to tell me, I—we could have been enjoying these wonderful kisses for months now?* she wanted to ask, but she wasn't bold enough, not yet.

"Well, aren't we a sorry case?"

He was right. Weren't they too old for these silly games? But then again, were they ready a couple of months ago, days ago, in fact? Who could tell? But now. . ."I guess that means we're moving on to the next step in this relationship." She broke her gaze from his. She wasn't sure she was ready to hear his answer.

"Are you as terrified about that as I am?"

"Yes and no. If we are meant to be a couple, Jared, God will guide us through this."

"I haven't felt these emotions since Hannah."

"Tell me about her, Jared." Alex handed him a sandwich and one for herself. "Please, tell me. She's a part of you, of your past, who you've grown into. I want to know her."

"She was just a kid. I suppose I was too, for that matter. We met in college. It was love at first sight. I didn't do anything without thinking about her first. It was great, we had so much fun together. We decided to get married after I graduated from college. It seemed like the best plan at the time, but I would never recommend to anyone a two-year engagement. It's not healthy."

"Two years?"

"Two years, and a young man. You're a doctor, you know the combination. It was an incredible test of my convictions, but God was gracious and saw me through it. Two weeks before the wedding I went home to the Vineyard, while she returned to her home to prepare for the wedding." Tears welled up in his eyes. "I wasn't there when it happened. The call from her father, crying on the phone, was my darkest moment. I literally fell to my knees, held my sides, and screamed."

Alex stood beside him and held him in her arms.

"The pain was so intense. I felt guilty for not being there, angry that God would take her away from me like that. It just wasn't fair."

Gently she kneaded his shoulders.

"My parents were a big help. We went to the funeral, of course. The image of her lying in that coffin, so peaceful, so beautiful—I wanted to crawl in and be buried with her.

As far as I was concerned my life was over before it even started."

She kissed the top of his head. What else could she do? "I've never known that kind of loss. My heart aches for you Jared, it truly does."

"I'm afraid to love, Alex. I'm afraid if I give my heart to others I'll lose them. Do you understand?"

"I think so. But, Jared, you won't lose me."

"You don't know that, Alex, any more than I do. I want to go further in our relationship—goodness, I have no choice, I see you in the morning, during the day, and at night. You're always around me."

"What are you saying, Jared? You only care about me because I'm always around?"

"No, goodness no! I meant in my mind's eye. I can't get you out of it. You're always there. You're so beautiful, Alexandria. You've awakened me in ways I thought were long dead."

"You're a pretty handsome guy yourself." She wanted to tell him she loved him. Loved him for who he was and not what he looked like, but she was afraid the words would scare him off. She held back her heart and caressed his cheek.

"It's not just your beauty, Alex, it's your mind also—who you are, everything about you. You drive me crazy."

Alex chuckled. "Ditto."

Jared laughed. "We're quite a pair, you and I."

"As long as we're a pair, I think I can live with that."

"Alex, if I had my way I'd haul you to a justice of the peace and be married by the end of the day. But I'm not ready for that. I know I've got a lot of baggage with regard to Hannah and my parents. Can we take it slow and see where our relationship develops? Continue as friends, but allow ourselves some kisses, maybe a tender caress once in a while?"

"Sounds like a plan," she said through a grin, giving his favorite response. "Mind if we share another kiss, now?"

He took her in his arms, possessive yet tender. This time the kiss was more gentle, the driving passion under control. Just maybe she could handle the physical attraction to this man.

≈

When at last they parted from the kiss, she asked, "So where are you taking me?"

"Patience is not one of your virtues." He slid her hair behind her shoulders.

"I never said it was."

"New Bedford."

"New Bedford? Why?"

"Well, my dear, there's a great whaling museum there and I thought you'd like to see it."

"Love to! So you said earlier you would be sleeping on the boat—where is it that I'm going to be staying?"

"I thought we could get you a room at a hotel on the water. Hopefully one with a dock so that I can be close by."

"Sounds like fun. How long will we be staying?"

"Just one night. I figure we can head back late afternoon and get in just before dark."

"Great. So, are you going to teach me how to steer this thing?"

Happiness didn't come close to what Jared was feeling in his heart right now. The woman he was falling madly in love with was standing beside him, trying to conquer her fears; she wanted to learn how to steer. He helped her into the captain's chair. "Okay, see the compass there?"

Alex nodded.

"That's our heading. Now when you steer, it's just like a car, except with really loose steering. You'll see." Jared turned off the autopilot and stood back.

"Did you do what I think you just did?"

"Uh-huh."

Alex hurriedly grasped the wheel. "Oh dear, what do I do?"

"Just remember the heading, Alex. Keep the compass heading in the same direction."

She worked so hard to keep it on course. He wanted to laugh, but she was trying. He couldn't help but take her as seriously as she took the job herself. Man, did he love this woman! "Excellent, honey, you're doing excellent." He stood behind her again and her shoulders relaxed.

"How long does this trip take?"

"A couple of hours."

He noticed she was shivering. "Are you cold?"

"A little." She rubbed her arms to warm them.

"Did you bring your heavy jacket?"

"Yes."

"I'll get it for you. Is it in your overnight bag?"

"Yup, thanks."

Something was so right in having her so close to him, in opening up his heart again. He wondered if he could keep it open, or if the years of shutting down and keeping out others would win in the end.

Down inside the cabin the air was warm. He opened her case and pulled out her jacket. It smelled like Alex. How he'd grown to love that scent. He peered out the porthole; they were close to the harbor now. Catching himself foolishly sniffing her jacket, he snapped the overnight bag closed and carried the jacket up to her. Their talk remained light the rest of the trip.

ᨠ

Walking the cobblestone streets by the whaling museum drew Alex back to a time far more rustic. Still, it was hard to picture this harbor in days of old with all the modern factories and working wharves on it. She enjoyed the museum well enough, but the best part was just spending the day with Jared. They had moved to a new level in their relationship, and she knew that the words the elderly woman spoke on the plane were coming to pass. "In God's time, everything will work out."

Jared talked of Hannah and his relationship with her. He filled in all sorts of details about what they did on their dates, where they liked to eat. They had been college kids back then, and they'd acted and lived the part. For her part, Alex hadn't told him yet about Peter and how he had broken her heart, but she figured she could save that for another day. Today they were beginning their own relationship; she didn't need to mar it with her ugly past.

ᨠ

The first month after their trip to New Bedford flew by in a blur of romantic evening meals, long walks along the shore holding hands, and occasionally yielding to their kisses. They played endless games of rummy and chess. Though he still lost to her consistently, his knowledge of chess ever increased.

Around the middle of May, Jared finally launched his boat. The name for the boat remained a constant inner battle for him. *Hannah* had always been a possibility, but somehow it didn't seem right with his relationship with Alex budding. *And what was it budding into?* he wondered. If he didn't watch himself, they would be an old married couple without the actual license. Every evening they spent together until bedtime, every day they assumed the other would just naturally be there.

This could be a dangerous thing, Jared worried, often taking the concern to prayer. "I accept my physical attraction to the woman, Lord, and I like her company, but I'm not ready to marry. I'm scared to death of it. I know, I know I'm supposed to trust You, but how can I? Everyone I ever loved has been taken from me. Pretty soon Alex will be packing her bags to go back to Kansas. I can't live in Kansas, Lord. And she's a doctor, she has patients back there. They are depending on her to return to them in a few months. It's not right. We can't, I can't, ask her to leave her life and join me in mine."

What was he going to do? He had already lost his heart; her leaving would completely rip it apart. And yet he couldn't take her career, her patients, her business away.

Alex's parents were due to come in a couple of weeks, during the early part of June. Jared worked feverishly to finish the boat before they arrived. The sails had come the week before. Some of the rigging still needed to be placed on the deck. The mast had been set a couple weeks back, thanks to the help of a few friends.

Jared let out an ear-piercing whistle. Captain charged toward him. "Hey, boy, where's Mommy?"

The dog barked as if he understood the question.

"Is she coming down here?"

The dog barked twice. Jared looked up the cliff. There she stood, her tall slender frame that fit so perfectly beside him silhouetted against a sea of blue sky. *But it will never work, she's got to go back.*

"Tell Alex I'm busy boy, go on. Shoo!"

Slowly the dog ambled off the dock, his nails clicking on the boards as he made his way to shore. Jared knew he was in a foul mood and he had no business taking it out on the dog. "Come here, Captain. I'm sorry."

The dog ran back and jumped on the deck of the boat. "Woof!"

Jared marveled at how the dog loved being on the boat, as if *he* were the captain. "Sorry, fella, but on this boat, I'm the captain." Wagging his tail, the dog soaked up Jared's attention, raising his hind quarters for a deeper petting.

&

"So what was that all about?" Alex stood with her hands on her hips. Something was bothering Jared. She had never seen him push Captain away before.

"I've just been having a bad day."

"What's wrong?" He was tense, his back as rigid as the mast.

"Alex, I don't want to talk about this now."

"So, it has something to do with us?" She searched his eyes for answers. He hid them from her scrutiny.

"Woman, are you a mind reader or something?"

"Or something. Jared, I read you like a book. From on the cliff I could tell something was eating away at you. That's why I sent Captain down. Figured seeing him would cheer you up."

"He did, sort of."

"You're doing it again, Jared."

"What?"

"Closing down."

No matter how much it hurt, she was going to see him through this. Maybe he would never be able to totally open his heart to her, but for as long as she had left on the Vineyard she was going to fight for him to break free at last.

"Me! Goodness, Alex, you've got something tucked away

so deep inside of you, you won't let me in either."

"Me? When did this become about me?"

"Look, honey, I don't want to argue. Please, just drop it."

"Jared, we can't keep doing this. Every time there's something we aren't comfortable with we stop talking. That's no basis for a relationship."

"What relationship? You're going home in a couple of months. Where does that leave us? What's the point, Alex? You've got your life, I've got mine. Maybe we're just too old."

Old? He thought she was old? *Doesn't he know I'd leave my practice and start one here? But I can't, not if he won't let me into his heart.*

"Who was he, Alex? Who hurt you so bad you won't tell me about it?"

Every muscle in her body tensed. She had wanted to tell him about Peter, she had intended to, actually. But the right time never seemed to present itself. Or maybe she just didn't have the right words.

"You say I'm closing down, I've closed off my heart," he persisted. "Well, honey, there's a piece of your heart you've never let me into. Not even a glimpse."

"Jared, I wanted. . ."

"Wanted what? For me to lay all of my life before your feet, tell you all of my wounds so you could use them to cut me off from probing into your own?" Jared stood in front of her and held her shoulders tight. "I know I'm right, Alex, whether you admit it or not. You are the one with the heart that has closed down. Trust me, I know what it looks like."

Tears burned at the back of her eyes, but she refused to cry. She wasn't going to show any weakness, not now. She'd won the battle with Peter, she had gotten on with her life. Such as it was.

"Fine, don't tell me then."

Within seconds he was on the shore walking away from her. Her heart was breaking. Why hadn't she told him about Peter? Why had she waited so long?

But she had waited too long. His heart was closing again; she'd seen it over the past few days. Verbal jabs about anything and nothing routinely passed his lips. He hadn't kissed her in nearly a week. He was pulling away.

Maybe it was time to return to Kansas. The tears fell freely now; her cheeks stung with the salt. "Come on, Captain, I think I'm going to pack."

The climb up the stairway in front of the cliff took forever; every step felt as though she were lifting a load of lead. She needed her entire concentration to focus on moving one foot in front of the other, to climb up the stairs, away from the sea, away from her captain. Some escape this trip to the seashore had been. She had made a wreck out of her life and the life of another. "God, I was right the first time—I was meant to be single. Why on earth did I ever believe there was hope for Jared and me?"

fourteen

"I need to leave for a few days," he told himself. She was everywhere. He couldn't breathe without catching a whiff of her scent. Her presence so flooded his soul it was mind-boggling. He knew what he had said to her was right. Perhaps he didn't say it right or bring it up at the best time, but someone had hurt her. *She doesn't trust. She gives of herself constantly, but doesn't trust someone to come in and hold her heart.*

He loved her, he knew it with every salty, briny section of his being. But she was right, too: A relationship has no foundation if one or both can't trust their hearts to the other.

"Well this is fun, Lord. I open myself up and get slapped in the face! You brought a woman into my life who has so much damage done to her that she can't open up and talk about it." Jared rattled around in the kitchen, picking up a cup and placing it down a few inches away, not really preparing to cook, not even doing the dishes, just expending mindless, useless energy.

He sat in his cottage all evening, until around three in the morning when he finally went to bed. He fought with himself to go and talk with her again, argue if he had too. Something needed to break in this relationship, or it was over.

ஐ

A persistent rapping at his door drove him out of his bed grumbling. The early morning sunlight made him blink.

Alex stood before him with reddened eyes.

"Captain will be much happier here with you." His back went rigid at the sound of her cold and controlled words. The dog walked through the opened door. Alex pivoted sharply and left.

"Alex!" *What is going on here? Wake up, Jared, the woman is leaving, and she's leaving the dog with you.*

Her shoulders stiffened but she continued to walk away.

"Alex, we need to talk."

She didn't respond. She was shaking now, grasping her sides, but still walking away from him. Away from "them" and any possible hope for a future.

"You're running away!"

Again no response; her pace quickened.

"For pity's sake, woman, don't do this!" Jared ran out the door and grabbed her in his arms. She stiffened like a board. He caressed her cheek. "Alex, please, can't we talk? Where are you going?"

"Home."

Jared's body tensed.

"I was wrong, Jared. I never should have gotten involved with you."

"Why? Because I'm forcing you to look at something in your heart that hasn't been resolved, in the same way you made me face myself? I don't think that's fair, Alex."

"In my case, things are different. It is resolved. It's over. Everything that happened between Peter and me is over."

At least I got his name out of her. That's something. "Honey, I don't think it's over."

"I haven't seen the man in seven years. Believe me, it's over, Jared." Her anger gave her strength. She pushed away from his embrace.

He tightened his hold, perhaps a little too tight. Her eyes lit with fear. His stomach heaved—she had been attacked. This Peter character had attacked her. He knew it with every ounce of his being. His heart softened. All his cruel words felt like ballast, sinking him further away from her. "Alex, I'm taking you into my place where we can sit down and talk this out."

She shook her head no.

"Honey, I don't know what that creep did to you, but I know one thing for certain, and deep down in your heart you know it too. I will never force myself on you."

Tears welled in her eyes as they darted back and forth. She was reading him, trying to figure out how he knew. "You know, don't you?"

"I suspect the man forced you in some way, am I right?"

The tears flowed down her cheeks now and she sniffled out a "yes."

His hold around her became more protective, firm but gentle. Then he scooped her up in his arms and brought her back into his cottage. Placing her on the couch, he squatted in front of her. "Can you tell me about it, Alex?"

"Oh, Jared, I was such a fool."

He caressed her chestnut hair and placed it behind her shoulders, wiping her tears with his thumbs. "Shh, none of that. If he took advantage he was the fool, not you."

"I should have seen it coming."

"Why? Honey, a creep like that is very manipulative in attracting people. You had no idea that in his heart he was ugly and not much of a man."

To this day she still blamed herself for what happened. Jared was right, though: Peter was a master of illusion. "Why couldn't I see?"

"Tell me about it, everything, and maybe I can help you sort it out."

"I wanted to tell you since the trip to New Bedford. I figured I would someday, but you were right, I kept putting it off."

"I should have been more patient. I'm sorry."

Alex proceeded to tell Jared about her relationship with Peter, how he used her from the start, at first wanting her to cover for him and his lack of studies. Then, the final night of their relationship, he tried to force his way on her. She blamed herself, too, because she had been tempted, wanting to explore some of her own sexual desires.

He held a finger to her lips. "No, love. The man was wrong. When you said no, he continued to press. That's when it was his fault and not yours."

"But don't you see, I wanted to for—a little while."

"Honey, we all want to at one time or another. It's how we control those desires that makes us successful against temptation or defeated by it. Alex, you've dealt with rape with your patients—what do you tell them?"

She felt a light bulb go on in her head; she had never applied her knowledge to her own experience. "They are the victim, they may have made a mistake, but the perpetrator is the one who was responsible."

"See, you know it here." He tapped her temple. "Now apply it here." He pointed to her heart.

"How?" Of course she knew the answers for her patients, but she had been unable to get past this for the seven years and more it had been haunting her.

"Forgive yourself for one thing. Your only mistake was being a poor judge of character, which in these cases is always difficult."

"I know, but. . ."

"What's the problem, Alex? Why haven't you released this stuff? You know all the psychological information regarding abuse and such. So why do you think you haven't moved on from Peter? Did you date after the attack?"

"No. Like you, I retreated into my own world."

"So what are we going to do about it?"

"We?"

"Yes, you have your baggage, and I have mine."

"I suppose we have to trust God, trust Him to forgive, trust Him with our hearts."

"Right. So how do you propose we do that?"

"I don't have a clue. We're a sad lot, you and I."

"Maybe. Or maybe we're just more honest than a lot of folks. We didn't bury our feelings and go into meaningless relationships afterwards, trying to find what we lost. Instead we separated ourselves until we were ready to deal with this."

"Are you ready to put Hannah aside and allow someone else in?" *Oh, Jared, I love you with all my heart, but I'm still afraid to tell you that,* she thought, probing his face for his answer before he gave it. She searched those deep, dark blue eyes she'd grown to cherish.

"I want to Alex. I thought, no, I believe, I have been doing it. The mere fact that I would allow myself to get involved with you at all is evidence of that."

"I've let you in too. But that doesn't seem to change the fact that we've both been holding onto pieces of our past."

Jared got up and sat beside her on the couch. "Alex, we took a big step today. You've shared something with me that you've shared with no one else. Let's not push ourselves too hard too fast."

"I'm going back to Kansas, Jared."

"I know. Will you be staying here for the summer—or are you leaving now?"

"What would you like?"

"Personally, I want you to stay here the rest of the summer. That will give us more time to heal and possibly get closer."

He's not ready to simply throw the relationship away. He did fight to have this conversation today. Maybe I should stay and see if there is more between us. Maybe I need to heal before I can completely trust another. Remember, you are the one who wanted to run. He wasn't running, he was waiting. Besides even if I wanted to go home today, I'm in no condition to drive halfway across the country.

"I'll stay for now, but I won't promise the rest of the summer."

"Fair enough." He stood from the couch. "Now, let me get to work. I want to have the boat ready for your folks." Jared took her in his arms and hugged her. She longed to hear him proclaim his love for her, but nothing came. He was a man who held tight reins on his heart. *Can I survive this, Lord?*

❧

In the days following they shared many more heart-to-heart discussions, learning to trust each other, themselves, and the Lord.

Finally the boat was ready, everything was done. Jared planned for her maiden voyage, but one thing still remained. The name. He couldn't believe he was, after all this time, not content with any name that he had come up with. He thought of naming it the *Alexandria,* but it seemed too noble a name for a work boat. And somehow *Alex* just didn't fit either. Many evenings he and Alex went over all sorts of names, from A to Z, up and down the alphabet, searching through literature, the Bible, old movies, anything and everything. Nothing stuck. And yet Alex, and everything about her, seemed so interlocked with the boat. He even thought of calling it *Dorothy* because she came from Kansas. And, like Dorothy in the Wizard of Oz, Alex had tried escaping from her life there.

His hand glided along the tiller, the varnish smooth as glass beneath his touch. He had sanded and sanded again, applying many layers, then buffed to a high gloss. Scanning the boat from bow to stern, he smiled with approval. She was a good vessel, rugged and sleek. The waves tapping against the hull made a rhythmic, slapping sound.

Alex came down the cliff, her every movement captivating his heart. How was he ever going to deal with her departure in a month? During their visit, he fell in love with her parents, and while he wanted to take them on a sail, he decided the maiden voyage would be the two of them alone. There was so much he still wanted to talk about, and yet there were always interruptions. The hospital had taken to calling Alex whenever someone was going on vacation. More days than not she was working, frequently long, hard hours.

Captain would stay with him during these times, but as soon as he heard her Bronco pull up, he was prancing at the door to go see her. Often Jared was jealous of the dog's close contact with Alex and his ability to have no inhibitions about running up and kissing her. "Lord, she's beautiful," Jared muttered as he waved to her.

Alex smiled and returned with a hearty gesture. She was wearing jeans, a cotton shirt, and a sweater tied around her neck. "Fine looking vessel, Captain." Her eyes sparkled with excitement, lit up with the June sun glistening off the ocean.

"Why thank you, ma'am. Would you like to come aboard?"

"May I?" She fanned her hand over her chest.

Jared roared. Her imitation of a southern belle dressed in jeans was so contrary. He took her hand as she stepped on board. "You look wonderful, Alex," he said.

"Aye, you ain't so bad yourself, Captain," she winked.

"Southern belle to pirate, without batting an eye. You're multitalented, my lady."

Alex laughed. "Honey, I deal with children—I need to be diversified."

"I reckon so." Jared pulled her to himself and kissed her tenderly. "I've missed you. You've been working a lot."

"I know. Remind me later I have something to bounce off you. But let's get going, I can't wait to have my first sail."

"Your first and her maiden voyage—only fitting."

"You still haven't named her yet?"

"Nope, but I'm working on it."

Alex wagged her head. "When you do come up with the name, it's going to be a good one. Nobody takes this many months to name a boat."

"How do you know?" Jared teased.

"Hmm, I'll have to ask around and verify my hypothesis."

"Okay, let's shove off then. Time's a-wasting, and the sun will be setting in a few hours."

❧

Alex sat in the stern and watched as Jared released the lines and pushed the boat into deeper water. He pulled the mainsail up to the top of the mast and secured the line on the cleat. She had learned so much about the boat, working on it with Jared. Lines, sheets, cleats, and winches were a part of her everyday vocabulary now. He stood beside her, pushing the tiller over to the left to catch the wind.

The whipping of the sail evened out as the wind filled it

and pushed the boat forward. It was so quiet on the water, nothing at all like the rides on motorboats.

"Alex, we're going to tack soon. When we do, you shift from one side to the other. I'll say 'ready about,' and if you're ready you say, 'ready.' Then I'll say, 'hard to lee' and you shift positions, okay?"

"Sure, but why?"

Jared smiled. "Because, my dear, that way everyone on board is prepared for the shift."

"But why those terms?"

"Well 'ready about' means, is everyone aboard, or 'about' this ship, ready. And 'hard to lee,' means we are moving to the lee side of the boat, the side that is sheltered from the wind."

"Gotcha."

"Ready about?" Jared watched the bow.

"Ready!" Alex stifled a giggle.

"Hard to lee." Jared pushed the tiller away from him and the boat spun to the right. The sail flapped loudly until it filled with wind again. Alex managed to scramble from one side to the other. Her heart raced. This was fun! She marveled at how easily Jared pointed the bow and the sail filled.

He pulled the tiller toward himself and the sail started to flap. "You didn't say 'ready about'!" she protested.

"Nope, this is called 'falling off.' It allows you to slow down the sailboat."

"Awesome. How did you learn all this stuff?"

"Honey, I've been sailing since I was in diapers. My mom was afraid I was going to grow gills."

"Oh, Jared, stop it. You're such a tease."

"Want to try?"

"I can't sail, Jared."

"Sure you can. I'll teach you." Jared patted the bench beside him.

Alex slid closer to him. "What do I do?"

"Here, hold the tiller."

She grabbed the tiller and Jared let go.

"Okay, push away from you."

She did, and the boat veered in the opposite direction. She panicked. "Jared, grab it, I'm going the wrong way!"

He placed his arm around her shoulder. "No, dear, with a tiller you do the opposite of where you want to go."

"Oh."

"Pull it toward you now." She did. "See?"

"Yes. . .this is so strange."

"I know, but you'll get used to it. Now look at the forward corner of the sail."

She stared at the white sheet. It was flapping a little, not full like when Jared was sailing. "Why isn't it tight?"

"Because you're falling off. Point the bow into the wind."

She pulled the tiller too hard and too close. The boat jerked and turned to the side. "Jared, help!"

"Relax, you simply pulled to hard. Ease off, that's it. Great, honey, you're doing great."

"I'm terrified."

He worked his strong hand over her shoulder muscles. "Trust me, you're doing just fine. You'll be a sailor in no time."

Alex watched the sail, scanning the horizon, staying alert.

"I like your folks," Jared said. "They're great people."

"Thanks, I'm kind of fond of them myself."

"What do they think of the island?"

"They love it. They think they're in paradise."

"Well they are, aren't they?" He nibbled her ear.

"Jared, behave."

"Sorry, you're just so irresistible."

Alex was more relaxed now and reclined in her seat. "It's a gorgeous day."

"Perfect." He was staring at her, examining her up close, making her feel so loved and adored. If only she could tell him she loved him.

The hospital had offered her a position today. They wanted to hire a pediatric physician as a part of the medical team for the Vineyard. The offer was tempting. She'd take it in a flash if she knew she and Jared had a future together. When they were together and not thinking about jobs, careers, futures, it seemed so right. He seemed to be an extension of her. But when he brought up her career, the atmosphere between them always became tense. He had made it clear on more than one occasion he'd seen enough of the world. The Vineyard was his home and he wasn't leaving it.

She searched his eyes—so deep, and brightened by the sun.

"So, do you like the quiet of the sea?" he asked.

"It's great. Very tranquil."

"I love it. It calms me down. It's my escape from pressures. It's like the waves take my troubles away."

Alex could feel that too. She wanted to ask him about their relationship. Did he want to go farther? Or was he content with her moving back home in a little over a month?

"You're doing great, honey. I want to go up front and check some lines. Just keep pointing into the wind like you've been doing, okay?"

"I don't know if I'm ready to go solo."

"You've been doing it for thirty minutes all by yourself. You can handle it, I'm sure of it."

She nodded. She was too nervous to speak. Every cell in

her body stood at attention. Every hair was raised like an antenna, alerting her to potential trouble. *Trouble, how do I know if there's trouble? I don't know what I'm doing.* Gnawing her lower lip, she tried to stay focused.

As her confidence was building, a speedboat crossed their bow very close, raising the bow of the boat out of the water. As it dropped back down, the boom bucked. She watched Jared, in the bow, grab for a line. He missed. "Oh Lord, no!" she screamed, "Jared!"

fifteen

"Oh dear God in heaven, let him be all right." She saw him splashing to the surface of the water. "Thank You, Lord."

He was waving at her, yelling something.

"What do I do now?" Her hand trembled on the tiller; Jared was getting further and further away.

Fall off, Alex, fall off, but how do I do that? She was trying to remember Jared's instructions. Her mind raced, her fears raged. She pulled the tiller toward her, and the boat turned too far to her right. She pushed the stick away from her and the boat started to go sideways.

Panic-struck, she stood up. Jared was swimming toward her. She leaned over the side, her knee pushing the tiller away from her some more. The boat was turning around. "Thank You, Lord."

"Jared!"

❧

"Oh, dear Jesus, no!" Jared swam as fast as he could. Alex was standing in the boat; danger hung in the wind. She was tacking; the boom was about to hit her in the head. "Get down, Alex!" he yelled.

He was certain she couldn't hear him. His chest aching, he propelled his body harder than he had ever done before. The thudding sound of her skull being nailed by the boom sickened him. *Don't think of that now*, he berated himself. *I've got to get to her, and fast.*

He kicked harder, reached farther, straining with each

161

stroke. The boat lay idle in the water, gently rolling in the waves. He caught a glimpse of her floating face down in the ocean. "Oh God, no. Don't take her away too! Please, God, let me save her. Help us. I love her. Please!"

Tears poured from his eyes. He reached her and lifted her head out of the water. He held her in his arms, kicking hard to keep them both above the surface of the waves.

"Alex! Please, Alex, breathe!"

He turned her around and placed his arm across her chest. He fought his emotions and forced himself to concentrate, trying to remember the lifesaving course he had taken as a kid. Covering the distance to the boat seemed to take forever, yet that was an illusion, he knew, and he continued to press on. When he reached the boat he pushed her body up so it draped over the stern. Then pulled himself on board. He noticed a small pool of water under her head. "Please, Lord, let that be from her lungs."

He grabbed her lifeless body and laid it tenderly on the deck. His body trembled with so many emotions. *She can't die, God, please don't take her away now! She's far to important to me*, he pleaded.

CPR, clear the passage ways. Come on, Jared, you can do it. He pinched her nose and blew fresh air into her lungs. "Come on, Alex, breathe, woman. I love you. Don't you die on me now! Breathe!" he yelled.

He worked on her for what seemed to be an eternity, though in reality it took only a couple of seconds. She coughed.

"That's it, baby, breathe, come on."

He rolled her to her side and rubbed her back.

She was breathing now.

"Thank You, Lord."

"Jar. . ." She coughed again.

"Shh, honey, it's all right, you're safe now. Everything is going to be all right." He kissed her forehead and cried.

They sat there, exhausted, the boat adrift in the middle of the ocean, its lines clapping against the mast. Minutes passed with no words.

"What happened?" she asked.

"You tacked and the boom hit you in the head, knocking you overboard." She felt the back of her head for the lump.

"Yes, my dear, you will be going to the hospital to have that looked at."

"But you were in the water too." She looked up to him and he explored her eyes. The pupils were dilated, but slowly responding to the sunlight.

"Shh, Alex. God was good. I was able to get to you. Relax." Jared's body quivered, the shock of nearly losing her overwhelmed him.

"Hold me, Jared." Her voice, raspy and hoarse, steeled his senses.

He gathered her into his arms. *I can't let you go, Alex. You mean too much to me.* He brushed her soggy hair away from her face. Her breathing was evening out.

❧

Alex savored the strength of his arms, the warmth of his chest. The thumping of his heart, still working hard, told her he was frightened. She had been frightened, too, but no matter what, she had to tell him how she felt. "Jared."

"Hmm?"

"I need to tell you something." Her voice grated past her lips. Her mouth could barely shape the words.

He held her tighter and rocked her back and forth.

"When you went overboard. . ." The tickle in her throat made her cough again.

He lifted her chin and his lips descended to hers. The kiss was tender; she felt so loved. "I love you, Jared." There. At last she had said the words.

"I love you, too. Alex, I can't live without you!"

Alex wept. How was it possible to love someone so much?

"I'll even move to Kansas, if that's what it takes for us to be together," he offered as a whisper in her ear, his breath warm and soothing.

"No, my love. Remember I had something to tell you?" She searched his eyes.

He nodded.

"I've been offered a position at the hospital and it will allow me to start my own practice here."

"When?"

"Today."

"You mean you'd live here with me?"

She nodded her head and wrapped her arms around him. "Only on one condition."

"What's that?" He eyed her curiously, pushing her back a little to see her face.

"Well," she let the word linger for a moment. "It isn't proper for a lady to ask." She traced his jaw with her fingertip.

"Oh! Well, I don't know. . .that's asking a lot, you know."

She playfully punched his shoulder. "You!"

"First, let me ask you, how do you feel about kids?"

"I love them, of course. Why else would I be in pediatrics?"

"Hmm, so you wouldn't mind having a few of your own?"

"Few! How many are we talking?"

"Well, I never told you this but twins run in my family."

"Twins, huh?"

"Yup." He toyed with the corners of her mouth, his feather-light touch sending an electrical charge over her skin.

"What if we just take them as they come and negotiate along the way?"

"Hmm, sounds like a plan."

"So, are you going to ask me?"

"It's a possibility."

"What?" They were playing a game; she loved him and she loved him for it.

"Now, Alexandria, a woman of your social graces knows there is a proper time and place for everything."

"Don't give me that. Marry me or I go back to Kansas."

"Is that a proposal?" he asked.

"Nope, that's a threat."

"Well, then, Dr. Alexandria Rose Tucker, would you do me the great honor of becoming my wife?"

"Yes."

He smiled and captured her lips once again. Alex was certain she would never get enough of this man's kisses if they lived to be a hundred and two.

"I've got a name for the boat, honey. If you approve."

"What's that?"

"*Sea Escape.* You came here to escape on the sea; I find the sea an escape from my stress. And here, right now, we've escaped from the bonds of our past. What do you think?"

"I like it. But you're going to have to teach me to sail. I don't want our children sailing circles around their mother."

"Hey, your folks are here. Why don't we get married right away?"

"And where are we going to spend our honeymoon?"

"Right here on the sea, my dear."

Alex laughed. "Of course, what was I possibly thinking? Sounds like a plan."

epilogue

Six Years Later

Alex bent over in pain. She knew this feeling, remembering two other times when she had experienced it before. "Michael Thomas! Mommy needs you."

A small golden-haired boy ran into her bedroom. "I'm here Mommy. What's the matter?"

"It's time, the baby is coming. Could you go get Daddy?"

"Okay. Mommy, can I come to the hospital this time?"

"No honey, I need you to help Papa John and Nana Martha watch your sister."

"But, Mom, I want to go," he pouted.

A sudden sharp pain attacked her, not even five minutes after the first one. She grasped the bed frame and supported herself. "Honey, if you don't run and get Daddy, Mommy isn't going to make it to the hospital."

His eyes widened with fear. "Mommy, are you okay?"

"Yes, honey, but I need you to go now, please."

"I'll get Daddy, Mom." Alex had never been so proud of her son. At five, he was growing into quite a little man. She reached for the phone and placed a call.

"Hi, Martha. It's time."

"Goodness, Alex, John just pulled in the drive. You've got great timing."

Alex chuckled. "I'm not sure. The contractions are coming

about five minutes apart. I hope we make it to the hospital."

"We're on our way."

Alex heard the phone slam down before the line went dead. John and Martha Poole had become dear friends and adopted grandparents to their children.

❧

"Daddy! Daddy!" Jared saw Michael running toward the dock.

"Hey, son, what's up?"

"Mommy. . ." He gasped for air. "Mommy. . .baby!"

"Mommy's going to have the baby?"

Little Michael vigorously nodded his head.

Jared dropped his power sander, turned off the generator, and scooped Michael up. "Let's go, son."

"Daddy, why does Mommy hurt?"

Jared was not ready for this question. His mind worked hard for a good honest answer that wasn't too revealing. Thinking was difficult when he needed to get to Alex. But his son needed answers. "Michael, when mommies have babies, it hurts them a little but it's only for a while and then there's no more pain."

"Mommy will be okay?"

"Yes, son, Mommy will be just fine."

"Did Mommy hurt when I was born?"

"Yes."

"And Megan too?"

"Yes, son." Jared was on the porch opening the door. There Alex stood with the bag for the hospital all packed. "How far apart?"

"Four minutes."

Concern gripped him. Alex's labor for Megan had only

been three hours. "Honey, are we going to make it to the hospital?"

"I hope so, but I don't know."

His knees locked. God would get them through this. "Do you want to stay here to have the baby, or risk getting to the hospital on time?"

"If John and Martha get here right away, I think we have time."

As if on cue, Martha ran through the door. "How far apart now?"

"Four minutes," Alex repeated.

"Papa John!" Michael ran into John's arms.

"You two get going, we'll take care of the kids." Martha ushered them toward the door.

"Thanks," Jared said as he grabbed the bag.

"Mommy!" Megan ran to Alex and grabbed her at the knees.

Jared picked his daughter up and held her tight. "Pumpkin, can you do Daddy a favor?"

Megan nodded.

"Nana Martha needs help making a special treat for Mommy and the new baby. Can you help her?"

"Okay, Daddy." Jared's heart tightened. In his daughter's eyes he saw so much love. He hugged her close and passed her over to Martha.

"Thanks, honey. Mommy and I will be back real soon. 'Bye."

❧

Alex winced at each and every bump they went over as Jared made their way out the dirt road. "Jared!"

"Are you okay?"

"Yes. No. Honey, can't you avoid the bumps?"

He took her hand. "I'm trying, dear. Relax. Have you started your breathing?"

"When did I have time?" Alex felt her temper rising. She knew her anger had to do with the labor and tried to fight her emotions.

"We'll breathe through the contractions together, dear."

"Sorry."

"Honey, I understand."

She wanted to snap at him. He didn't have a clue what she was going through, but she fought off the urge.

They made it to the hospital in record time. She didn't want to ask Jared how fast he was driving.

"Dr. Madeiras, good to see you. Is it that time?" the receptionist asked.

"Yes, stat!" Alex called out.

The receptionist placed a call and the door flung open to a man pushing a wheelchair. She and Jared were ushered to maternity.

❧

The pain was gone the instant the doctor proclaimed, "It's a boy."

Jared kissed her. "He's beautiful, Alexandria. Have I told you lately that I love you?"

"Not in the past few minutes," Alex beamed. "I love you, too."

Alex held her newborn son up to her breast, and he began to suckle. Jared wrapped his protective arms around them both. "Thank You, Lord, for another blessing, and another to love. Bless him one day with a woman as wonderful as his mother."

A tear formed in Alex's eye. Seven years ago she had left

Kansas, convinced God was calling her to a single life. And yet His plans were a mystery, at the time, to her. The frumpy old lady's voice on the plane played back in her mind, "They that wait on the Lord, dear. . ."

Ah, those homemade,

comforting family dinners around the table. But who has time to make them between carpooling and softball games?

Don't let your busy schedule deter you. This collection of delectable recipes—from the readers and authors of inspirational romances—has been gathered from all over the United States, and even from Greece and Australia.

There are tried and true recipes for every occasion—Crock-Pot meals for busy days, fast desserts for church dinners, rave snacks for after school, holiday gifts for those picky relatives, and much, much more. Over 700 recipes await you! Bring back the joy of treasured moments over good food with the ones you love. So, dust off the china and treat your loved ones (and yourself) to some delicious home cooking.

The Heart's Delight *cookbook has what every family needs—cooking from the heart.*

400 pages, Paperbound, 8" x 5 ³⁄₁₆"